# The Mystery of the Gingerbread House

D0964911

Illustrated by Frank Aloise

# The Mystery of
# the Gingerbread House

## Wylly Folk St. John

AN AVON C CAMELOT BOOK

*This book, with love,*
*is for the real Ronny and Greg—*
*and their grandparents.*

AVON BOOKS
A division of
The Hearst Corporation
959 Eighth Avenue
New York, New York 10019

Copyright © 1969 by Wylly Folk St. John
Published by arrangement with The Viking Press, Inc.
Library of Congress Catalog Card Number: 69-13802
ISBN: 0-380-01731-8

First Camelot Printing, August, 1977
Fifth Printing

CAMELOT TRADEMARK REG. U.S. PAT. OFF. AND IN
OTHER COUNTRIES, MARCA REGISTRADA, HECHO EN
U.S.A.

Printed in the U.S.A.

# Contents

The Secret in the Basket 7

The Case of the Missing Grandmother 25

The Conjure Woman and the Bad Guys 49

A False Lead and a New Clue 68

The Boxwood House and the Man Upstairs 86

The Hospital Clue 99

The Man with the Stolen Cars 118

The Key Under the Frog 137

The Clues in the Manuscript 157

The Rocks in the Trunk 170

The Clue at the Cemetery 185

Inside the Gingerbread House 199

*Other Avon Camelot Books by*
**Wylly Folk St. John**

| | | |
|---|---|---|
| THE SECRET OF THE SEVEN CROWS | 51763 | $1.75 |
| THE SECRETS OF THE HIDDEN CREEK | 45765 | $1.50 |
| THE SECRET OF THE PIRATE INN | 46318 | $1.50 |
| UNCLE ROBERT'S SECRET | 46326 | $1.50 |
| THE MYSTERY OF THE OTHER GIRL | 48207 | $1.50 |
| THE CHRISTMAS TREE MYSTERY | 46300 | $1.50 |

WYLLY FOLK ST. JOHN is a true southerner. She was born in South Carolina, spent her childhood in Savannah, graduated from the University of Georgia in Athens, and is now living in Social Circle, not far from Atlanta. She was employed as a staff writer for the Magazine Section of the *Atlantic Journal and Constitution* for many years.

# The Secret
# in the Basket

What's that?" Greg said.

Ronny looked where his brother pointed, and gasped, and looked again.

They were moving with exaggerated caution around the corner of the house, trying to stay out of sight behind the azalea bushes. It was just after daylight. They had slipped out early this August morning to follow Mr. Hambrick, their next-door neighbor, to the shopping center nearby, where he owned a restaurant.

Mr. Hambrick left at that hour because he had to be at the restaurant early and he liked to walk; he hadn't done anything criminal. It was just that Ronny felt he and Greg could use a lot more practice in tailing people without being noticed, if they were going to be real detectives. Yesterday Mattie, their maid, had caught them at it, when they tailed her to the bus stop. She had seen them and told them to go back or she'd stop at the pay station and call their mama. That proved, Ronny had told Greg, that they needed a lot more tailing practice. Greg was only ten and believed everything Ronny said, because Ronny was twelve.

But now Greg even forgot to watch for Mr. Ham brick to come out of his front door, because of some-thing he could see on their own front steps. He said excitedly, "It looks like—"

Ronny frowned, concentrating. Nothing like that had been there the night before when Mama called them in because it was bedtime. During vacation they were allowed to stay out after supper until dark. There was a good game of kickball going on under the light at Ted Halverson's drive, but they had to leave when Mama called. They had raced each other up the steps to the porch, and there had been nothing at all on the steps, Ronny remembered.

He said, "My dear Watson, I deduce from the basket with handles that it is used for carrying something. You probably did not notice, as I did, that it has a sort of pink blanket in it. I deduce from this—"

"It's a baby!" Greg said bluntly. Then he remem-

bered to add, panting, "My dear Holmes." They were both running for the steps by now, forgetting to stay under the cover of the shrubbery. Mr. Hambrick came out of his house and walked at his usual leisurely pace down his drive, whistling "The Caissons Go Rolling Along," without the boys even noticing him.

They stopped short, staring at the basket.

"It's asleep," Greg whispered. "I think."

"Elementary, my dear Watson," Ronny said, bending over to poke an experimental finger into the folds of the pink blanket.

"Don't—you'll wake it up," Greg said.

"I want to wake it up." Ronny poked harder. "I want to see if its eyes are open yet. If it hasn't got its eyes open yet, I can deduce that it's an extremely young child, my dear Watson."

"It already looks pretty young, to me."

"You aren't using scientific detecting methods, like I am, my dear Watson. You're just making a snap judgment."

"Sorry about that, chief."

"No—you can't be Max Smart and Watson too. Besides, I'm Max, when we're fighting Kaos."

"You're always everybody that's any good," Greg grumbled.

"That's because I'm older. When you're twelve you can be anybody you want."

"You'll still be older."

"I expect I'll be going with girls or something by then. But right now—"

"Okay, okay. —Look, its eyes are open!"

"Blue," Ronny said.

The baby opened its mouth, too.

"It's howling," Greg said. "Let's take it to Mama."

"You know what she said about that stripedy kitten we brought home," Ronny said doubtfully.

"She let us keep Froman, though."

"Froman's a good watchdog, and Dad said every home could use a good watchdog. But you know how Mama carried on about No More Pets, unless they're small enough to go in the goldfish bowl or the turtle dish."

"This one's little all right," Greg said, "but I don't think—"

"Elementary, my dear Watson." Ronny picked up the basket—he could carry it in one hand—and Greg opened the front door.

"Ma—ma!" he called. "Hey, Ma—ma!" They always hollered *Mama* as soon as they got inside the door, whether they needed her for anything or not.

"I'm in the kitchen," Mama called back. "But don't get in my way now—you know I've got to get your dad's breakfast so he won't be late for work."

Their father was a Captain in Special Services, an Army career man now stationed at Fort McPherson. They lived in West End, a section of older Atlanta about twenty minutes' drive from the Post. Dad said they could move onto the Post as soon as one of the red-brick houses for officers was vacant. But it seemed none of the other Captains would ever get transferred. Ronny and Greg would have liked to live on the Post, where they could see the marching every day, and Retreat every afternoon when the flag came down, and the parades on Fridays when the band played, and go to the Post movies and the Post swimming pool just by running across the parade ground instead of getting on a bus.

But, as Dad said, the house on the Post was something to look forward to. It was always good, he told them, to have some little thing to look forward to—otherwise you'd be sunk. You'd be at The End. Greg wasn't sure he understood that, but Ronny thought he did.

Now they rushed into the kitchen, both talking at once, and the baby crying. Ronny put the basket on the counter where he usually put the groceries when he helped Mama unload the station wagon.

"You take whatever that is right on back outside—" Mama began.

Then she saw what it was.

"Help!" she hollered, and Froman got up from his corner and started barking, to help her. "Rob! Come here quick—they've brought in a baby—from somewhere! A baby— What next?"

Dad came running, with lather on his face and his razor in his hand. "All right—where did you guys get a baby?" he demanded. "Gosh, Dorinda, it's a—a small one, isn't it?"

"Brand new," Greg said proudly.

"Well, not exactly brand new," Ronny said, correcting him. "It does have its eyes open."

"They all have their eyes open," Dad told him. "Newborn babies aren't like kittens."

"No kidding?" Greg said with interest. "Even when they're inside their mothers?"

"Right," Dad said. But Greg thought he looked a little doubtful about that bit. "Now, men, where did this one come from?" He looked at Mama and then at the baby, and said, "Pink—was that for boys or girls?"

"Girls. It might be a girl." Mama picked up the baby out of the basket and cuddled it in her arm.

"I deduced that already," Ronny said. "Elementary, eh, my dear Watson?"

"Right, Holmes."

"Cut out the Baker Street stuff, will you, guys, and come to the point," Dad ordered. "Where—did—this—infant—come—from?"

"We found it on the front steps," they answered together. Then Ronny said, "Can we keep it, huh, Mama?" Greg added, "We never have had a pet girl before, you know."

"I'm going to finish shaving." Dad left hurriedly.

"Chicken!" Mama called after him.

"One time I heard you tell G. M. that you wanted to have one more baby, because we needed a girl," Ronny said.

"But G. M. said you seemed to have your hands full, with us," Greg said. "So you didn't have it after all. At least not yet."

"You boys don't miss a thing, do you?" Mama said. "Your grandmother and I must have thought we were having a private conversation."

The baby had stopped crying and was moving a little pink hand toward Mama's face.

"It's waving at me," Ronny said.

"Its nose is running," Greg pointed out. Mama reached for a tissue and wiped the nose. Then she said distractedly, "I've got to finish breakfast. No, of course you can't keep it, boys. It belongs to somebody. We'll have to call the police—but right now I've got to finish breakfast." She put the baby back in the basket, and it began to cry again.

"It's hungry, too," Ronny said. "Can I feed it, Mama?"

"Wait till I get your dad off, and I'll see."

Ronny said, "Hey—I know where there's a baby bottle. We had it to feed Billy when he was a baby goat, remember, Mama? And when you made us let him go off to live at that farm I kept the bottle to remember him by, and just in case we ever had another baby goat named Billy or anything."

"All right—get it and clean it thoroughly," Mama said. Ronny observed with interest that she was fast losing her cool. "Hot water and soap. Then we have to sterilize it. You can put it in that boiler—but keep out of my way, will you? I've got to hurry. Where in the world is Mattie? She would be late—on a day like this!" She started beating the eggs—a little harder than she usually beat them.

"Boy—wait till Mattie sees what we've got!" Greg said, gloating.

"I only hope she won't turn right around and go back home," Mama said. "We'll have to tell her right away that we aren't keeping it—or she might quit."

"Aw, why aren't we keeping it?" Greg coaxed. "You know you'd just love a sissy girl baby with long hair to curl and put hair ribbons on." Mama didn't even bother to answer.

Ronny came back with Billy's bottle. "You just wait," he told the wailing baby. "I'm doing it as fast as I can. You don't want to get Billy's germs, do you?" He washed the bottle and set it to boil, along with the somewhat worn nipple, while Mama put the food on the breakfast-room table.

"You boys come on," she said. "Rob—breakfast!" she called, and Dad came in, looking keen in his uniform, ready to go except for his jacket and cap.

"You haven't put it out yet?" he said, kidding.

He always took time to hold Mama's chair for her before he sat down.

"We haven't even fed it yet," Ronny said reproachfully. The boys pulled up to the table and folded their hands in front of them.

"Your turn to say grace," Greg told his brother.

"Thank Thee, Lord, for breakfast," Ronny said dutifully, and then added with a soulful glance upward, "and thanks for the pet baby, too."

"It's a conspiracy to wear us down," Dad said to Mama, who was pouring his coffee. "Remember to stand firm against all their strategy, will you, please?"

Mama got up, saying, "You all go ahead and eat. I'll warm some milk."

Ronny was through his breakfast—though he hadn't chewed it very much—by the time the bottle was ready. "Let me—" He stood beside the counter and leaned over the basket.

"All right," Mama said. "Hold it at an angle, see—"

"I know how to do it," Ronny told her. "You forget I fed Billy all the time he was a baby."

The baby grabbed thirstily at the bottle with her pink mouth.

Greg urged, "It's my turn now. I want to feed her too."

"You can be the one to change her," Mama said, laughing. "I'll find something that'll do for diapers, temporarily. Maybe tear up an old sheet."

"I don't want to change her diaper!" Greg backed away fast. "Ronny can—"

"She's half yours and half mine," Ronny said. "I call the top half."

"We—are—not—going—to—keep—her," Mama reminded them.

Dad said, "Good-by. Let me know how you come

out. I'm thinking of requesting Temporary Duty in San Antonio or somewhere." He kissed Mama good-by and went out the door just as Mattie came in.

"Lord have mercy!" Mattie said. "What's that?"

"Haven't you ever seen a baby before, Mattie?" Greg said kindly. "It's ours—she belongs to Ronny and me because we found her—but you can be the one to change her diaper if you want to."

"She's gone to sleep," Ronny said wonderingly, "before she even finished eating."

"Poor little thing," Mama said. She told Mattie, "The boys found the basket on the front steps. Yes, I know it sounds like a soap opera—but that's what happened. I'm going to call the authorities just as soon as I have time. But I'd better find something for diapers first. I know she needs changing."

"Let's go outside and play," Greg suggested to Ronny fast.

Ronny said, "You watch her, huh, Mattie?" and beat Greg to the door. Greg grabbed the kickball from the back hall and sent it whizzing down the drive.

"Hey—who's that?" Ronny said.

A girl was standing on their sidewalk, looking toward their house. She had a crutch under her right arm, and as the ball rolled toward her, she kicked it with her crutch and it flew toward the boys. Ronny caught it. "Hey—that's pretty good!" he said. "For a girl." He didn't say for a girl with a crutch. After all, anybody could break a leg and have to use a crutch. Only this kid hadn't broken a leg. She had a brace, like polio-poster kids wore.

"Yeah," Greg said admiringly. "That's cool. Let's see you do it again."

"Kick it to me, then." The girl hopped nimbly to where the ball was rolling and gave it a good whack with her crutch.

"First time I ever saw anybody kick a ball that way," Ronny told her. "You want to play kickball with us?"

"Sure."

"What's your name?"

"Evie. Evelyn Hollis. I'm nearly thirteen, in case you want to know that too."

"I'm Ronny Jameson and this is Greg. I'm nearly thirteen too. Greg's ten."

"I'm as near eleven," Greg said, "as you're near thirteen, Ron. Did you have polio, Evie?"

"Yes. When I was three. Anything else you want to know?"

"Let's play!" Ronny shouted. "You take it from me and Evie, Greg."

They were panting and blowing when they sat down on the steps after a while to rest.

"Where do you live, Evie?" Greg asked. "You didn't go to our school."

"I live over on the other side of the shopping center," Evie told them. "We moved there after school let out."

"Oh," Ronny said. The other side of the shopping

center wasn't such a good place to live. He had heard
Mama say all those houses were going to be torn down
before long, in the slum clearance project, whatever
that was. Still, Evie was a sharp kickball player. Her
clothes weren't bad, and her face was clean. She had
clear brown eyes kind of like Froman's, and straight
dark hair, and a good tan with a spot of red on each
cheek. He liked her. Where she lived didn't matter.
But Mama probably wouldn't let them go over to Evie's
house to play, he thought gloomily.

"Hey," Evie said casually, moving a twig around on
the bottom step with the tip of her crutch, "have you
kids got a baby brother or—sister or—anything?"

"Well—sort of," Ronny said doubtfully.

"Not exactly," Greg said. "She's not really—"

"Why?" Ronny said to Evie.

"Well—" Evie kept on moving the twig around with
her crutch. "I thought maybe your mother might need
a baby-sitter, and I'm a real good baby-sitter, and—"

"Why not?" Ronny said. "Mattie's probably too
busy."

"Can you change her diapers?" Greg asked earnestly. "Because that's one thing—"

"But anyway, Mama's going to call the police about
her—we just found her this morning—so we won't
need a baby-sitter very long."

"Oh, no!" Evie stood up, her cheeks getting redder. "Let's go ask your mother if she won't let me take care of her, instead. Hurry!"

Ronny didn't see what the hurry was, but he opened the door for Evie and hollered, "Mama!"

"Hush," Mama said, coming into the hall. "You'll wake the baby. Oh? Who's this?"

"This is Evie. She wants a job, baby-sitting."

"Hello, Evie," Mama said. "But how did you know we had a baby here?"

"I—I just thought you might," Evie said, stammering. Then, back in the kitchen, the baby started crying and Evie jumped. She started toward the sound. "Where is she? I can make her stop crying."

"Come on back to the kitchen," Greg said. "That's where we keep her."

Evie hurried. Ronny thought, I've never seen a kid run with a crutch before. Then he saw Froman, and he ran, too. Froman had his paws up on the counter—he was a pretty big dog, old Froman was—and his nose was pushing the basket where the baby lay. He had almost pushed it off the counter; it teetered on the edge.

Evie lunged at Froman with her crutch, and then snatched the baby up out of the basket and held her close. "Oh, Joy—Joy—" She was almost crying, Ronny noticed.

"Hey, what's the matter?" Greg asked her. "Froman wasn't going to bite her. He was just trying to get acquainted, I guess."

"How come you called her Joy?" Ronny said.

Mama said gently to Evie, "Your middle name wouldn't be Miriam, would it?"

"Yes'm—no'm—I mean—"

To his horror Ronny saw enormous round tears form in Evie's eyes and roll down her cheeks. He had never seen tears as big and distinct as those before. They were almost as big as clear glass marbles. Most tears were just wet spots.

"Don't cry, Evie." Greg shoved Froman back into his corner. "He won't bother you."

"Yes'm," Evie confessed to Mama, still holding the baby. "I did think I could do like Miriam in the Bible story. She put her baby brother Moses where some real nice people would find him, and then she got a job with them, baby-sitting, so she could watch over him. So I—"

"This is your baby? Your little sister?" Mama asked.

"Yes'm. Her name's Joyce, but we call her Joy. Because that's what she is," she said a bit defiantly.

"She's a real good baby. She's not a bit of trouble. I see these kids lots of times—and you and sometimes their daddy—over at the shopping center, and one time I followed you home, just to see where you lived. Because you looked like a—such a nice family. And then—when I had to run away and hide Joy—well, I thought maybe—well, Miriam in the Bible story got away with it." The big tears came up in her eyes again. Ronny reached for the box of tissues and handed her one.

Mama said, "But, Evie, why? Why did you think you had to hide the baby? Where's your mother?"

"In the hospital. She got hit by a car and she's unconscious."

"But—your father?"

"He's dead."

"Then—where are all your other relatives?"

"That," Evie said, with trouble all over her face and her lips quivering and the round bright tears spilling again, "is a mystery."

# The Case of
# the Missing Grandmother

Mama put her arm around Evie's shoulder and hugged her, and then took the baby while she nudged Evie into a chair. "You sit right down there and eat some breakfast," she said, "while you tell us all about it."

"Good thing you hadn't called the police yet, isn't it, Mama?" Greg said. "Now we know who the baby belongs to, we won't have to call them at all. Evie and Joy can both stay here with us."

"We'll see," Mama told him. "Since their mother's in the hospital, that might be a good thing for them to do, if there's nobody else to look after them. But we'll have to find out—maybe their mother's better by now." She placed the baby, now asleep again, back in the basket, and told Mattie to put her in the bedroom where it was quiet. Mattie could listen out for her while she straightened up the house.

Then Mama filled a plate generously with breakfast for Evie, who said, "Thank you," before she started eating hungrily.

"Evie likes scrambled eggs—even cold," Greg observed.

Ronny said sympathetically, "How bad was your mama hurt?"

"Mrs. Garner next door—I hate Mrs. Garner!— called up the hospital and they said she was in a coma, and Mrs. Garner said she might—not live." Evie's tears came again, and she put down her fork, swallowing hard. "She's got to live!" she said fiercely.

"Do you know which hospital?" Mama asked kindly. "I'll call—maybe she'll be all right."

"Grady Hospital. Please—would you—?"

"Of course. I'll do it right now, before we do anything else. What's your mother's name?"

"Mrs. Lewis. Mrs. Christina Lewis."

"She doesn't use your father's first name or initials?"

"No'm—he's dead. She doesn't use Finch's either."

"Finch?"

"Joy's father. Finch Lewis. We ran away from him before Joy was born."

"Why?" Greg hadn't learned yet about being tactful, Ronny thought. But Evie didn't mind answering.

"He was mean. He hit Mother—he was always trying to make her give him something she had. He and his mean old brother—a guy named Crane Lewis— wanted to sell whatever it was for a lot of money. She wouldn't give it to him. And I think she couldn't stand it that he stole things."

"Stole!" Ronny said.

"Cars." Evie shook her head, "I think. I used to hear Mother begging him to stop, and not to go out with Crane any more. He wouldn't, so we left."

Mama shook her head, too, and went into her bedroom to telephone—Ronny figured that was in case Evie's mother had died or anything. But she hadn't. Mama came back and said Mrs. Lewis was still unconscious, but, "I left word, when she wakes up, to tell her the children are safe and staying with us. I told them our address and phone number, and they'll get in touch with us if there's any change in her condition."

Ronny suddenly went and hugged his mother. "I knew it—I knew it," he whispered.

"Knew what?" She disentangled herself, after hugging him back.

"You're letting them stay with us. I knew you would. You're such a good Mama." It sounded like he was laying it on thick, but he meant it.

"Flattery will get you nowhere." That was what Mama always said when the boys tried to be ingratiating. "I couldn't do anything else. It's what I'd want somebody to do for my children if I were unconscious in a hospital." This reminded her, though, that she hadn't found out Evie's whole story. "Evie, isn't there somebody we ought to call about your mother? And you two children? What did you mean about your relatives being a mystery? Where are you from?"

"We came from California right after school was out," Evie told her. She stopped crying and was now drinking her milk slowly, enjoying it. "We lived in Verde."

"Then your relatives are in California?"

"No'm. We didn't have any—out there."

"Then where?"

"I don't know," Evie said. "I know it sounds crazy, Mrs. Jameson, but my mother never would tell me who they are. She wouldn't tell me who she was before she was married. She said she'd destroyed everything that could possibly let anybody know, ever."

"Why would she want to do a thing like that?" Greg asked.

Evie shrugged. "All I know is, her name is Christina Elizabeth. And I think—I think I have a grandmother, and I think she lives in Atlanta somewhere, and I think that's why Mother wanted to come back here. I think she wanted to be near my grandmother even though she didn't want her to know it. It sounds crazy. I just wonder all the time about it. But I don't really know. It's pretty awful not to know."

"It's terrible," Ronny agreed earnestly. "Not to know your grandmother! Greg and I couldn't stand not knowing G. M."

"We sure couldn't," Greg agreed. "G. M. is the greatest. Grandpa's pretty nice, too." He wanted to be fair about it. "And if we could see our other grandpa and grandma sometimes I'm sure they'd be real good guys, too," he added politely. "But it's G. M. we depend on. Right, Ron?"

"Right."

"Well, I've just got to find my grandmother now," Evie said, and she looked sort of desperate—white around the mouth—and frightened. "Because that old Mrs. Garner said they'll take Joy away from me if—if Mother doesn't get well, and put her in a foster home, and put me in a different place, if we don't have any kinfolks to take care of us. I couldn't stand that. That's why I had to hide her from Mrs. Garner. Joy's my baby—I've watched after her ever since she was born! She's mine—and nobody's going to get her."

"You mean—her father?" Ronny guessed.

"Finch." Evie nodded. "I hate Finch. And I'll take care of Joy all right. Nobody's going to take her from me—even if he has a right to. But I just know my grandmother would love to have us, if I could find her. She's rich."

"Great," Ronny said. "But how do you know she's rich?"

"Oh—I just know. From things Mother said when she didn't realize it. And there's a photo album, of pictures from when Mother was a girl. Her house is in it. A beautiful great big house. If only I can find her—Mother's mother—I know she won't let Mrs. Garner tell anybody to take Joy away from me."

"They won't do that," Mama said. "I'll telephone Mrs. Garner and explain to her that you and Joy are staying with friends until your mother gets well. We'll need to go and get your clothes, of course."

"But if she doesn't get well—"

"Don't think about that now. Just pray that she will." She ruffled Evie's hair with a gentle hand.

"If your mother were conscious," Ronny said

thoughtfully, "and knew how much you need to know,
I bet she would tell you your grandma's name and
where she lives."

"Sure she would. But—she might not ever get conscious enough to tell me."

"Let's go out and play," Greg proposed. He was getting tired of all the sadness.

"Well—" Evie considered. "If Joy's asleep and
doesn't need me to baby-sit—"

"That's all right," Mama said. "Mattie will hear her
if she cries. You go on out with the boys."

"Come on," Ronny said, holding the back door open.
"We'll show you No. 221B Baker Street. You can be
Miss Morstan. I'll go up first, my dear Watson."

"Quite so, Holmes." Greg stood back while Ronny
climbed to their tree house—a platform they had
built between two low spreading limbs of a huge oak
tree. Their dad had helped them nail crosspieces to
the tree trunk to make steps.

Evie said, "You're the only kids I know besides me
who read Sherlock Holmes. Hardly anybody would
know who Miss Morstan was. But I do. She's in *The
Sign of Four*."

"Big deal," Greg said amiably. "Our dad likes Sherlock, too. Lots of people watch him on TV. They're
having reruns now. Basil Rathbone."

"Now let Miss Morstan come up," Ronny said. Momentarily he abandoned the character to say, "I forgot about your crutch, Evie. Can you climb the ladder if Greg boosts you and I pull?"

"Sure I can. I can do anything you can do," she bragged. "It just takes a little longer." She dropped the crutch and put the foot with the brace on it on the lowest crosspiece, bringing her other foot up to the next. It wasn't easy, but they tugged and pushed until they had her aloft. Ronny knew it was somehow important to her to be able to make it. He couldn't let her fail.

When they were all three seated around Sherlock's study, with their backs against the various tree branches, Ronny said, "We'll take the case, Miss Morstan. Eh, Watson?"

"Quite so, Holmes. Uh—which case?"

"The Case of the Missing Grandmother," Ronny said solemnly. "If anybody can find Miss Morstan's grandmother, we can. Gosh, Greg, don't you see what a wonderful chance for detecting this is?"

"Yeah," Greg said, getting excited too. "Sure! And it's so important, too."

"It's vital," Ronny said emphatically, "for Evie to find her."

Evie looked more hopeful than she had all morning. "It sure is," she agreed. "And maybe you kids really can help me find her. If all of us try very hard."

"State your case, Miss Morstan," Ronny said.

"He means, tell us all about yourself, Evie," Greg said, interpreting.

Ronny said, like Sherlock, "Beyond the obvious facts, Miss Morstan, that you are very nervous, that you belong to the library, and that you have very poor eyesight, I know nothing whatever about you."

"My dear Holmes!" Greg said. "This is too much. I'm—what was that word, Ron—baffled. My eyes are as good as yours, but I don't know all those things about Miss Morstan. I fail to see how you worked it out."

"It is simplicity itself," Ronny said, still in Sherlock's words. "You see, my dear Watson, but you do not observe. Miss Morstan mentioned reading about a certain famous detective; yet she is not rich and probably doesn't own the book. Therefore I deduce that she goes to the library. She bites her fingernails; hence my deduction that she is nervous."

"You'd bite your nails too," Evie remarked darkly, "if you'd had the things happen to you lately that I have. If you had Mrs. Garner to escape from."

"And," Ronny went on, "she has a white button on

her shirt sewed on with black thread. Therefore I deduce that she has poor eyesight, since she can't tell white from black."

"Wrong," Evie said. "We just didn't have any white thread, that's all."

Ronny gave up the stiltedness of his Holmes role, and said eagerly, "Evie, tell us everything you can remember, that would give us any clue to who your grandmother is and where she might live."

Just then Mama came to the back door and called, "Evie, do you know this Mrs. Garner's initials? And what's the street address?"

"Mrs. B. C. Garner," Evie answered. "Ashby Street. I guess hers is 110 because ours is 112."

"I'll call her and tell her not to worry about you."

"Thanks, Mrs. Jameson," Evie said gratefully.

"Now about your grandmother," Ronny said impatiently. "We've got to get to work right away. We've got to find her before—"

"Before anything worse happens to my mother." Evie nodded soberly. "Well, let's see. If we go back home for our clothes—and Joy does need her diapers —we can get the picture album. It shows the house Mother lived in, and there are pictures of her and her parents and brother and some of her friends. There's one taken·in front of the school—I've wondered if I could recognize that school if I happened to see it. I know I'd recognize the house."

"But this is an awful big city," Greg said. "You can't look at every school and every house in it."

"Anyhow, it doesn't show all of the school," Evie said with discouragement. "Only the front. Say, though—I just remembered. A picture of Mother as a cheerleader has a B on her sweater! That could be a clue."

"Great!" Ronny applauded. "Think of some more. Didn't your mother tell you anything about when she was growing up, or little things about her mother, or her brother, or anything that would help?"

"Sure she did. She told me lots of things—off and on—mostly when she forgot and didn't realize she was telling me. But it's hard to think which ones might be important. Let's see now. It was a big white two-story house with curlicue wooden lace all around the top of the porch and around the banisters—she said it was called a gingerbread house back in Victorian times. The wooden lace was called gingerbread because it looked like the white icing on gingerbread cookies. Lots of houses had it for decoration. And there was boxwood in the front yard, and stained-glass panels at the sides of the front door—she used to look out and see the trees through the red and blue parts, and they looked like red and blue trees, and the sky through the green part, and it looked green. And there was a staircase with a landing where she used to play dolls, that had a stained-glass window, too. The colors were in diamond shapes.

"And the house had a yellow rose vine growing all across one end, that she said was called a Lady Banksia rose, and it was just covered with the most beautiful roses in spring. Oh, yes, and the house had at least one old-fashioned fireplace. There's a picture in the album of Mother when she was about my size, in a long dress—she said it was her first formal—standing by the mantel with her face reflected in the mirror. It was one of those mantelpieces that had a mirror set in over the fire part, between two dark wooden columns."

"I never saw one like that," Ronny said.

"I'll show you the picture when I get my mother's album."

"What else do you have that could be clues—things she had when she was a girl living at the gingerbread house?"

"Well, there's this." Evie pulled on a chain that hung around her neck, and a small medal on the end of it came out from inside her blouse. "She lets me wear it. It's a medal she won when she was in high school, for writing a history essay for the U. D. C. contest. My mother is a writer, but editors don't have enough sense to buy what she writes, very often; so it doesn't bring in much money. I wish I had some talent."

"Well," Greg said comfortingly, "you sure know how to cry pretty good."

"It's my only talent, though. Unless you count wiggling my eyebrows. See?" She lifted an eyebrow and twitched it.

Greg said respectfully, "Wish I could do that. Even Ronny can't—he can only wiggle his ears. I can't do either one. But I can throw my thumb out of joint." He showed her.

"That's great," Evie said.

"Aw, you're just saying that to make me feel good."

"Maybe so. But what's wrong with making people feel good? I always do if I can."

Greg thought that over, and nodded. "Hey—I believe you're right."

Ronny said impatiently, "Let's get back to business, you kids. Let me see the medal, Evie."

She pulled it over her head and handed it to him. It was between the size of a nickel and a dime, of dark-red enamel on a gold disc, with a leaf design around the edge. A shield in the center had an engraved *U. D. C.* intertwined, and '61–'65. Surrounding the shield, engraved letters read, *For excellence in history*. Ronny turned it over, but the back was smooth gold. He said disappointedly, "Sometimes prize medals have the name of the winner engraved on the back. I thought maybe her name—her last name when she was in high school, I mean—was on it."

"Silly—I'd've known if it were," Evie said. "Then all I'd've had to do would be to look in the phone book and call up everybody with that name and ask them if they ever had a daughter named Christina Elizabeth."

"What does U. D. C. mean?" Greg wanted to know. "And '61–'65?"

"It means United Daughters of the Confederacy. It's like a club, see, only to belong to it your father had to have been a Confederate soldier in the War Between the States. I guess it's mostly real old ladies now. The years they fought that war were 1861 to 1865."

"Maybe some of the old ladies would remember this particular medal—and remember her?" Ronny said thoughtfully.

"No. They had the contest every year, so there'd

have been lots of medals. Unless we knew her last name or which year or which school or something there's not much chance of finding out anything from this. Or she wouldn't have let me wear it, see?"

Ronny handed it back to her. "Well, it's a clue, anyhow. We've got to keep thinking how we can use it. What else do you remember that might help? Do you remember your dad? Maybe he had some relatives that would know your mom's family?"

"No. He died before I can remember. But he was a hero. My mother said he was drowned trying to rescue a little boy from the undertow at the beach. They were both swept out to sea and never found at all."

"But what about his family?"

"She said he was an orphan."

"Did she ever show you a clipping from a newspaper or anything about when he got drowned trying to rescue the kid?"

"No, but—see here, Ron Jameson, are you trying to make out my father wasn't a hero? I'm not going to stand for—"

"No, 'course not. I only thought maybe it would help. They always put 'He was survived by—' and then tell the relatives and the wife's born name and all."

"Well, there weren't any clippings that I ever saw." She frowned, a puzzled look coming into her eyes.

"Come to think about it," she said reluctantly, "she never had any pictures of him, either. You'd have thought she'd've kept a picture of him—if she loved him. She had a picture of her brother—my Uncle Sandy."

" 'Course," Greg said, "lots of mothers get divorces because they don't love their husbands any more. So they wouldn't hardly keep their pictures around. You reckon your mom got a divorce?"

"If she did," Evie conceded, "she never told me anything about it."

"Well," Ronny said, "right after lunch, let's go to Evie's house and see what clues we can find there. Aren't there some other things your mom had left from when she was a girl, besides the photo album?"

"A few. There's a bracelet and a silver-backed hairbrush, and they both have monograms on them, but the letters are so twined together I can't tell even what the last letter could have been, and she never would tell me. She would tease me sometimes when I begged, and say it was X or Z. But it wasn't. Then she'd say, 'It's U.' But it wasn't U either."

"Could've been for some name like Underwood, or —or Upshaw?"

"No—she was kidding. I guess I can tell when my mother is just kidding. The pictures, though—maybe you can deduce something from them that I didn't see, Ron."

"Come on. Let's go see what's for lunch," Greg said.

It was easier getting Evie down from the tree house than it had been to get her up the ladder. Ronny held her by the arms while she dangled down and Greg could reach her from below, so when she turned loose she didn't fall hard.

While they ate hamburgers and drank chocolate milk, Mama told them she had talked with the neighbor and convinced her that the children were staying with friends, though Mrs. Garner insisted at first on talking about Evie's "running away."

"She won't bother you, when you go to collect your clothes and Joy's things," Mama told Evie. "I'll drive you over there after a while."

"Can't we just walk over there, right after lunch?" Ronny said. "That's what we were going to do. It's just over on the other side of the shopping center."

"Well, I did have a Garden Club meeting this afternoon," Mama said. "Since Evie walked over here carrying Joy's basket—I guess you three could manage. But if there are too many clothes and things, Evie, just collect them and leave them where I can pick them up later. Do you have a key?"

"Yes'm, Mother let me carry the extra one. There aren't too many clothes. But I wish—sometime—I could get Mother's big trunk. If—if she's not going to—get well right away, I mean. It had something in it—"

"Oh, the trunk and her other things will surely be all right until she gets back home," Mama said. "Just get the clothes you and Joy need right now."

"Yes'm."

Evie insisted on feeding Joy herself, and changing her, and putting her to sleep, while Ronny and Greg stood around impatiently urging her to hurry.

"Okay, okay, I'm ready now," she told them at last. Ronny had his magnifying glass and a notebook and pencil; he let Greg carry a suitcase Mama lent them to bring back the clothes in. Evie had Mama's gardening basket and two paper sacks, also for collecting things.

"What's in that trunk you were talking about?" Ronny asked her as they neared the street where she lived.

"I don't know. That's another thing she wouldn't tell me. But I think it's important. She kept it locked all the time—I never, ever saw her open it—and I never saw the key. But it's got a big heavy lock you couldn't break. And it's a big thing—I don't believe we could move it even if we wanted to take it away. Unless we had two men to carry it, like the movers did."

"Did she bring that from home when she left here to go to California, all that long time ago?"

"I don't see how she could've. But she's had it ever since I can remember."

"Hey, Evie, do you live in a house or an apartment?" Greg asked as they turned the corner into Evie's street.

"An old house with a big old yard. It's almost hidden under a lot of cottonwood trees and stuff. Cottonwood trees are no good for anything. It's an ugly old house —I hate it. But my grandmother's is beautiful—if I could find it. This one's not really much of a house— hardly fit to live in. But the rent wasn't much either. And it's paid till the end of the month, thank goodness. See, we only had one of Finch's unemployment checks to cash after we got here, and there wasn't too much money, because my mother couldn't work on account of Joy being born and all. She tried writing things, but she didn't sell but one article all that time. It was to the Sunday Magazine in the newspaper."

"Which house? That one with all the plants and flowers and stuff in front?"

"No, that's Aunt Riah's. Ours is the next one. And

then Mrs. Garner's on the other side." She made a face at Mrs. Garner's.

"Who's Aunt Riah? Your aunt?"

"No, silly. I told you I don't have any relatives— any I know. Aunt Riah is a real nice old colored woman who's a conjure woman. She hid us from Mrs. Garner till it was just before daylight and I could take Joy to your house."

"What's a conjure woman?"

"Well, it's a sort of a lady witch doctor, only she does good witching mostly—kind of magic spells to help people, like to make them fall in love, or to bring them good luck. I guess she could put on a bad spell if she wanted to, though. She gave me a mojo to keep Joy and me safe and bring us good luck." She reached in the pocket of her shorts and pulled out a small bundle tied in a red rag. "Here it is."

"What's in it? I never saw a real mojo." Ronny held out his hand for it but Evie put it back in her pocket.

"Can't open it—that'd break the luck. But it's got some sure-enough conjure stuff in it. A piece of High-John-the-Conquer root, and a buckeye, and some other magic good-luck things."

"You don't really believe in that stuff, do you, Evie?" Ronny said.

"No," Evie admitted candidly. "But it's sort of like a

prayer, you know; it might help. It doesn't hurt anything, to carry a mojo. There's a thing called faith they tell you about in Sunday School. Whatever you believe is so, is, even if it can't be. Aunt Riah believes she's helping me; so it doesn't hurt to let her. You know as long as you believed in Santa Claus he was real and he brought your presents. When you stopped believing in him, he stopped bringing you things and it had to be your father and mother. See? Now this mojo might not do me a bit of good, but I'm not going to throw it away, because that would hurt Aunt Riah's feelings. And somewhere else in my mind than where I keep my real good sense I kinda want to save it anyhow, just in case."

"Okay," Ronny said. "Keep it, then. I used to carry a rabbit-foot myself, but I figured it brought me bad luck instead of good, because I lost it."

"It was the wrong kind of rabbit-foot," Evie said. "You have to get one that's the left hind foot of a rabbit caught in the dark of the moon in a graveyard, Aunt Riah says."

"No wonder," Ronny said. "Mine came from the dime store."

"Hey!" Greg said. "Is this your house? Look—somebody's been here and left the door open! And—and scattered things around."

Evie started to run, crutch and all, and the boys hurried to catch up with her.

"My dear Watson," Ronny said, "I deduce that there's been a burglary here."

# The Conjure Woman
## and the Bad Guys

Just look!" Evie said. "Somebody's torn up everything."

The front room was a mess. So was the kitchen. So were the two bedrooms. Toothpaste was spread around all over the bathroom. There wasn't much furniture, but if there had been any more the place would have been even more of a mess, Ronny thought.

Evie ran to her mother's room and came back sobbing with rage. "They took it. They took the photo album and her brush and bracelet and watch and everything."

"Did they take that locked trunk?" Ronny asked.

"No—it was too heavy, I guess. And they couldn't

break it open, either, thank goodness. It's still okay. And so is the picture. I forgot to tell you about the picture of her house she painted when she was just a kid." She pointed to it on the wall over the mantel— a water color framed in gilt, showing the white gingerbread house with trees around it and yellow roses at one end.

"What kind of trees are they?" Ronny asked. "That could help us identify it, if we knew."

"She said they were oaks and chinaberries."

"She wasn't too good at painting trees, was she?" Greg said critically. Then he added hastily, "But awful good at houses."

"She was just a kid."

"We'll have to take the picture later," Ronny said. "It's too big to carry, with all the other stuff."

"They didn't take your clothes, did they?" Greg asked. "And Joy's diapers and things?"

They hurried into the other bedroom.

"No—but look! They threw 'em all around. Dumped 'em out of the dresser drawers and messed 'em up. They were all folded nice—"

"Well, never mind. We can fold 'em up again." Greg started picking things up from the floor and putting them on the bed. Evie began folding them. Ronny was examining the front door with his magnifying glass.

"Observe this, Watson," he called. Greg grinned at Evie and went back into the front room. Ronny said, "The door has not been broken open. What does that tell you, my dear Watson?"

"Maybe it was already open?"

"I deduce that the one who entered had a key, or else was a professional burglar with tools to open doors."

"No," Evie said, coming in with the basket of folded diapers ready to take along when they left. "I'm afraid I forgot to lock it. And I had the key in my pocket, too! See, I was in a hurry and all upset because I heard Mrs. Garner saying what she said about me and Joy, and I wasn't careful about locking up. I could kick myself. I just grabbed Joy and sneaked out the back way and went over to Aunt Riah's. I knew Mrs. Garner wouldn't look for me there because she won't have anything to do with Aunt Riah. But of course I knew we couldn't stay there. It was just till everybody was asleep and I could take Joy away without anybody seeing us."

Ronny said, "My dear Watson, what does the flour scattered all over the kitchen floor tell us?"

"That they must've liked to throw flour?"

"My dear Watson, you see, but you do not observe.

Note the footprints in the flour. There are two different sizes. I deduce that there were two of the bad guys, one older than the other."

"And both bigger than any of us," Evie said. "They look almost like men's shoe prints."

"Here's another one—a smaller one." Ronny discovered it. "Big boys might—but men wouldn't—mess things up just for fun. So I deduce there were two big boys and one small one."

"Maybe Aunt Riah saw somebody over here," Greg suggested. "Maybe she saw who got in and did all this."

"Let's go ask her!" Evie said. "That's a real good idea, Greg. I want to tell her anyhow, that the mojo brought me good luck. Maybe it was the mojo—at least it won't hurt to let her think so."

"This is good luck?"

"Well, it was good about your mother liking Joy and —and letting us stay with you-all for now."

"What about all this bad luck?" Ronny looked around the disarranged room. "What about those clues that are gone? The things they stole?"

Evie said tensely, "We'll get 'em back! We've got to get 'em back! Or I might not ever find my grandmother. Come on, let's ask Aunt Riah if she saw anything."

Ronny and Greg had never seen a place like Aunt Riah's before, nor a person like the conjure woman. She was very old and brown and wrinkled, with grizzled, crinkled hair and deep-set, bright black eyes. Evie told them later that she had blue gums. All conjure women had blue gums—that was how folks knew when they were born that they could be conjure women. Ronny wished he could see her gums, but even Evie hadn't actually seen them.

The room smelled queer and different, but not bad. The funny fragrance was surely coming from the bundles of dried plants and stuff that hung all around the walls. They were plank walls, not papered or plastered or anything, but they had been whitewashed a long time ago. The fireplace had been whitewashed, too, but inside it was black with soot. It had no fire now, of course, but a black kettle and a black iron pot sat on the hearth. Ronny thought, She must cook up her witch-stuff in that. The bed in the corner had a patchwork quilt over it, made of all kinds of bright cloth scraps. Evie told him later that Aunt Riah called it a crazy quilt.

Evie hugged the old woman and then introduced Ronny and Greg. "My friends," she said. "Ronny and Greg Jameson. Joy and I are staying at their house. Mrs. Garner can't get us there, Aunt Riah."

Wiping her hands on her blue-checked gingham apron, Aunt Riah shook hands with each boy. "Set yourselves down," she invited. "I was just makin' me some sassafras tea. You all like sassafras tea?"

"I don't know," Greg said. "I never drank any. Did you, Evie?"

"Sure," Evie said. "It tastes good when it has lots of sugar. It's a pretty red color. You ought to try it."

"Okay," Ronny and Greg said together. "Thanks, we'd like some, Aunt Riah," Ronny added politely.

The conjure woman had blue oilcloth on her table, to match her gums, and she set out thick white cups and poured the clear, ruddy liquid for the children. Her sugar bowl was blue, too. Ronny watched Evie and put three spoonfuls of sugar into his cup, as she did. Greg did too.

"It's good," Greg said.

"Sure is," Ronny agreed, though he had tasted things he liked better.

"If you have the measles," Evie told them, "it brings out the bumps, so they won't go in on you. If they go in on you, you might die."

"We already had the measles," Ronny said thankfully.

Evie said, "Aunt Riah, somebody tore up our house and stole some of my mother's things that I need. We were hoping you saw them and could tell us who did it."

"I see 'em all right," Aunt Riah said. "And I put a spell on 'em. They got to give them things back."

"Who was it?"

"Bunch of bad boys lives across the street over yonder on the corner. Name Jowers. You know 'em, don't you, honey? Messin' 'round with old cars and nearly runnin' over people. Ain't got nothin' better to do than tear things up while their ma's out workin'. I hollered and told 'em to leave that place alone, but those boys didn't pay me no mind. So I put the spell on 'em."

"Why didn't you call the police, Aunt Riah?" Ronny said.

"Polices scared to start anything, times like this. 'Fraid they'll be a ruckus."

"But kids oughtn't to get away with doing stuff like that. My dad says it's just stupid, senseless vandalism —I think that's the word—to tear things up for no reason at all."

"Don't worry, they won't get away with it," Evie said grimly. "I'm going over there and get my stuff back."

"How big are they?" Greg asked practically of Aunt Riah.

"Bigger'n you are, son. Bigger'n Evie, too. You better stay away from there, Evie honey."

"You forget I've got that mojo you gave me, Aunt Riah. It already brought me good luck—when I picked out Ronny and Greg's house for Joy."

"Mojos is all right, but they's times when it ain't safe to lean on 'em too hard," Aunt Riah said.

"If you've got any stronger conjures, I'd appreciate 'em," Evie said. "But I'm going, anyhow."

"We'll go with you," Ronny said, not very enthusiastically. "Even if they are bigger than we are. How many of them are there?"

"Three or four," Aunt Riah said. "Two nelly grown, and two young'uns, I reckon."

Greg said to Aunt Riah, "Could you give me and Ron a mojo too?"

"Well, it takes time to make a good mojo. But I'll give y'all a buckeye. That'll help."

"Thanks, Aunt Riah." They put the buckeyes in their pockets and followed Evie out.

"Gee, I hope her spell works," Greg said.

Evie's mouth was set in a straight line and her chin jutted out. As she went across the street and toward the corner house, Ronny thought, She can march with a crutch too, as well as run with one. She's marching like a sergeant leading a platoon. Look at old Evie!

She swung herself up the steps of the ramshackle house where the Jowers boys lived. Ronny and Greg backed her up. Ronny had his hands in his pockets, but Greg had his fists clenched.

Evie pushed the doorbell, but they didn't hear any ring. "It's probably broken," Ronny said. "It looks like everything around here might be broken. Knock, why don't we?" He hit the door a couple of sharp raps with his knuckles. But he wasn't feeling very brave.

"Are you scared?" Evie asked Greg, because he looked white.

"No," Greg said. "But I might throw up."

"Don't worry; they won't hurt us," Evie said. "Kids that do mean things are usually cowards. They're the type. That's why I never tried to play with this bunch or anything since we moved here."

The door opened suddenly. Two boys taller than Evie or Ronny stood there. "What do you want?" one of them said.

He was tough looking, Ronny thought. His shirt was dirty, too. Maybe the rest of them weren't home.

Evie said hardily, "I want that stuff you took from my house, Bim Jowers. All of it. Right now."

"Oh, you do?" Bim Jowers laughed, a sneery sort of laugh. "Hear that, Toby? She wants her stuff back."

Toby laughed too. "Why would anybody want old stuff like that back? It ain't no good. Nobody would buy it. I don't know why we took such junk anyhow. That old bunch of pictures and all. Even the watch wasn't worth sellin'."

"You mean you tried to sell my mother's things?" Evie cried in outrage. "You—you—" She lifted her crutch and hit him with it, hard, on the head. It didn't hurt him; he laughed at her even more. "She's got guts, ain't she?" he said to his brother mockingly.

"Look," Ronny said reasonably, "if the things aren't any good to you, why don't you give them back? They mean a lot to Evie."

"What'll you do if we don't? Want to start something?"

"Well, I guess we'd have to fight you. But it would be better not to," Ronny said honestly.

"You're right it'd be better not to, for you," Bim said threateningly.

"Let's see you take 'em back," Toby said.

A big brown dog came from the back of the house and stood between the two Jowers boys. Bim put a hand on his head. When Greg saw that, he said to Ronny, "Look—maybe they're not such bad guys. They've got a dog sort of like Froman. Maybe, if we told them why Evie needs the stuff so bad—" He reached over and patted the brown dog on the head, and got a wag of the scruffy tail.

"Well," Ronny said, "it's worth a try. A guy that likes dogs can't be all bad. Would you listen a minute, you two? Evie's mother is in the hospital, see, and unconscious, and she might die. And Evie needs to find her grandmother, because if she can't, somebody might make her and her baby sister go to different old orphan homes or foster homes or somewhere separated, to live. And she has to keep her baby sister..

Her only chance is to find her grandmother. And the only way we can do that is to study the clues in that stuff that belonged to her mother when she was a girl, see? You got the photo album and some other things that might help us locate her relations. There's a picture of her grandmother's house and all. How about giving the stuff back? If you will, we won't go to the police or anything."

"Police!" Toby laughed again. "You bet you won't. You won't be able to go to any police." He made a chopping motion with his hand, like karate, and Ronny could almost feel it on the back of his neck.

But Bim said slowly, "Maybe we oughta go along with that, Toby. Remember when Ma was in the hospital that time when we were little kids, and they put us in that home and we had to run away? I kinda feel sorry for any kid that has to go to one of them homes."

"Maybe they could pay us for the stuff," Toby conceded. "You kids got any money?"

"No," Ronny said. "We didn't bring any money with us. But you couldn't make us buy it back, when it belongs to Evie."

"Want to bet?" Toby said. "We could make you, okay, if you had any money."

"Well," Greg said, patting the dog again and looking

up at the big boy who towered over him, "we don't have any; so it wouldn't do you any good to try. But we could give you each a lucky buckeye." He pulled his buckeye out of his pocket. "It'll bring you luck—especially if you give back Evie's things." He held out the buckeye to Toby—and Toby took it.

"No kiddin'?" Bim said. "You got another one?"

Ronny gave him his, thinking, How right Aunt Riah was. She said the buckeyes would help. Maybe her spell will work, too.

Bim went off and came back, bringing the photo album and a paper sack with the hairbrush and bracelet and watch and some other odds and ends in it. "Here," he said gruffly to Evie.

"Thanks," Evie said, not a bit gratefully.

Ronny had an idea. He remembered his father had once told him that it was odd, but if you let somebody help you, he feels more kindly toward you.

"Hey, maybe you fellows would help us?" he said. He opened the photo album and found the picture Evie had told him about, of the gingerbread house. "Did you ever see a house that looks like this? Because this is where Evie's grandmother lives. We hope she still lives there, because she's not the type that would ever give up the old family home. And if we could find it—"

The two older boys looked at the picture, and then at each other, and Ronny thought there was something strange and furtive in the way they acted after they saw it. They clammed up.

"No," Bim said, and Toby echoed hastily, "No, we never—"

"Well, if you ever do happen to see a house that looks like this," Ronny said, "please let us know." He wrote down his phone number on a page he tore out of his notebook, and gave it to Bim. "There might be a reward." He thought he might touch Dad for some money for such a good cause, if there wasn't enough in his bank and Greg's.

"Okay, okay," Bim said. "You kids better get lost now."

"Well, thanks," Ronny said. Greg patted the brown dog again, and said, "Good-by, boy," to him. Evie looked scornful and independent; she didn't even say "Thank you" again. Ronny knew the Jowers boys didn't deserve any thank yous; he could almost hear Evie thinking, Well, they shouldn't have taken my stuff in the first place. And besides, look how they messed up the house.

When they were back at Evie's, though, she did let on how glad she was to get her mother's things back. She showed them to Ronny and Greg, and her hands just loved the silver brush and the little bracelet and the old book of photos. The watch was a new one, not from her mother's childhood, but not worth enough money for the Jowers boys to keep it.

Ronny looked hard at the engraved initials on the brush and bracelet, but Evie was right—you couldn't tell what they were. "We'll look at all the pictures when we get back to your house," Evie said. "Right now I've got to clean this place up and get our clothes together."

"Let's get busy," Ronny said, and Greg started picking up again.

But Evie stopped in the middle of scrubbing up the bathroom to say to Ronny, "Bim and Toby Jowers know something." ·

"What?"

"Didn't you see how funny they looked when you showed them the picture of the gingerbread house? I bet any money they know where it is."

"I thought they did act funny," Ronny agreed. "Like they'd seen it or something. I thought maybe they'd tell us, for that reward I offered."

"If they won't," Evie said, "we've got to think of some way to make 'em."

"But how?" Greg said. "They look like they won't make easy."

Ronny had been thinking. "Surely you see what this means, my dear Watson?"

"No, I don't."

Evie cried, "Come on, Ron, if you've thought of anything, tell us!"

"It means," Ronny said, dragging it out for suspense, "that if they recognized the house, it's more than likely to be somewhere in this very neighborhood!"

# A False Lead and a New Clue

They showed Aunt Riah the snapshot and asked if she had ever seen the house, but she hadn't. She said she didn't get around much on account of her achin' joints.

"Well, we've got to get back, because Mrs. Jameson might worry if we're late to supper, and I have to tend to Joy," Evie said. "We've got the house all cleaned up, and I locked it good this time. Aunt Riah, if you should see anybody bothering it again, I wish you'd call the police."

"Honey, you know I don't bother no polices and they don't bother me. But I be glad to put another spell on anybody foolin' around over there."

"Spells aren't as good as police," Greg informed her kindly.

"That'n worked right good, didn't it?" Aunt Riah cackled a high laugh. "They give the things back, didn't they?"

"Well, look," Ronny said, again writing his phone number down on a page from his notebook, "could you go to a phone at the grocery store or somewhere and call us if you should see anything wrong at Evie's house? After you put the spell on, of course," he added so as not to hurt her feelings. "Because that trunk of Evie's mother's is still there, and it might have something important in it."

"I could do that, sure enough," Aunt Riah promised. "So don't you worry none, Evie honey. I keep a eye on yo' house."

"Thanks, Aunt Riah."

Greg said, "You wouldn't happen to have another couple of buckeyes, would you, Aunt Riah? They sure are handy good-luck things to have." He had already told her how they had used the buckeyes for bargaining with the Jowers boys. "In fact I don't think a guy should ever be without a buckeye in his jeans, in case he needs it bad."

"That's right," Aunt Riah said. "I give you each an-

other one. I got plenty—I knows where they's a buckeye tree in a graveyard."

"Wow! Thanks, Aunt Riah." They told her good-by
and hurried home, Ronny lugging the suitcase, which
was too heavy for Greg, and Evie the basket with the
most important things in it, diapers and the things of
her mother's, while Greg managed the two paper
sacks, stuffed with more clothes and diapers. Evie
wanted to bring the painting, but reluctantly agreed
she would have to leave it until next time.

As soon as they got home, Evie went to look at Joy,
who was still asleep, and then called the hospital to
ask about her mother. The boys waited while she
dialed, asked, and hung up slowly. " 'Condition unchanged,' " she said miserably. "Not good, I guess."

"Not any worse, though." Ronny tried to be hopeful.

After supper the three sat down on the living-room
floor to look at the photo album. Ronny had his Sherlock magnifying glass, which was proving itself very
useful for making out details in the snapshots.

"I can even see the diamond-shaped stained-glass
panes in the door," he said, examining a picture of the
girl Christina on the front steps of the white house.
"I can almost see the number on the post."

"It looks like 250 to me," Evie said. "I asked her

once what that number was, but she wouldn't tell me. She wouldn't tell me the name of the street, either."

"Your mother was pretty when she was a girl," Greg said.

"Yes," Evie agreed proudly. "She had lots of boy friends and went to dances and was a cheerleader. But she really liked to write better than anything. See, here's her picture in her first formal." The girl looking into the mirror had on a long ruffly dress, with a corsage pinned on her shoulder. "It was her first orchid," Evie said. "A boy named Tank gave it to her. He was taking her to the junior-senior prom."

"Was that his real name?"

"No. They called him that because his last name was Tankersley. His father owned a garage. She had another boy friend named Billy, at the same time, and he gave her a cashmere sweater for Christmas, and Tank gave her a string of real, sure-enough cultured pearls. The pearls broke later and she never did find them all. She didn't mind telling me things like that."

"She looks like she was a pretty good cheerleader, too, in this picture here."

"She did that all right, but she would really rather write. She got elected feature editor of the school paper for her senior year. And then she ran away and got married before she could be it. She looked kinda sad when she told me about that. I know she wished she could've been feature editor and graduated with her class. But if she had, where would I have been?" Evie frowned. "I often wonder."

"She didn't happen to tell you the name of the school paper?"

"No. Most all the time she'd remember to clam up just before she told me anything really important."

Ronny said thoughtfully, "Maybe your grandma and grandpa disowned her when she ran away to get married without finishing high school."

"Mother's father had died earlier. See, this is his picture, but it was made when she was real little. No, I don't think they would disown their own daughter just for getting married, do you? She was their only girl. She just had one brother, my Uncle Sandy. He was five years older than she was. She loved him a whole lot, I could tell, but she wouldn't talk about him much. She kind of choked up when she thought about him. About never seeing him for the rest of her life, I guess. Here's his picture—he played football, see?"

"Here he is in an Army uniform, too," Greg said. "Let's ask Dad which war he was in, huh?"

Their father figured it had to be the Korean War. That might have been 1952 or 1953, he said.

"Mother would've been around fifteen then," Evie

said. "Because she got married in 1955, when she was just seventeen."

"So your uncle would be about thirty-six now." Ronny was calculating it in his notebook. "If we could find him." He made a note: *Look for a thirty-six-year-old man—about the same age as Dad.* "What did Sandy stand for? What was his first name?" He asked Evie. "That would help, if we're ever going to find him."

"Gosh, I don't know. She never called him anything but Sandy."

"Dad, what could Sandy stand for?" Ronny asked.

"Oh, it could be for Sanders. Or Alexander. Or just a nickname because he has sandy hair. Let's see his picture." Dad studied the bareheaded one solemnly with Sherlock's magnifying glass and said, "Yep, he had sandy hair, all right."

"If it was Sanders," Ronny said excitedly, "he could have had a family name for a first name. Like, you know, my name is Ronald because Mama's born name was Dorinda Ronald. So maybe your grandma's born name was Sanders, Evie."

"I see what you mean," Evie said, "but that doesn't help us find her now. Because she would be under her married name in the phone book or anywhere. And

that's the one we don't know. My mother's born name
—that was my grandmother's married name." She
had another thought. "I just remembered," she told
them, "about how she used to phone. Sometimes she
would get so homesick she just couldn't stand it, and
she would dial her mother's phone number and wait
till she answered, just to hear her voice—or maybe
Uncle Sandy's voice, for all I know—and then hang
up without speaking. And then she would cry a little
bit. I used to try to see what number she was dialing.
After the area code, the first three numbers were 552,
but I never could get the rest."

"Maybe she was trying to get up nerve enough to
talk to your grandma, and just couldn't," Greg said.

"I know she was. Once when I asked her why she
didn't go ahead and talk, she said, 'I've got too much
pride.' That was the reason. But she wouldn't tell me
any more about it."

Mama said sympathetically, "False pride can hurt a
lot of people besides the proud one, can't it? Her
mother would want to hear from her, no matter what
the reason was she went away from home. If your
grandmother guessed your mother was the one making those phone calls and then hanging up without
speaking, she probably cried too."

"Ronny, get me the phone book," Dad said. "We can look in the front and maybe find out what section of town has 552 for an exchange."

It was a good idea, but it didn't work. Every exchange within the city limits merely had "Atlanta," though all the suburbs were identified with their exchange numbers. Dad was getting interested in the problem, now. "Maybe tomorrow I could ask someone at the phone company," he offered. "The offices are all closed now. But perhaps we could at least pin it down to some one part of town."

"That's a great idea, Dad." Ronny was elated.

"Thanks, Captain Jameson," Evie said.

Greg was still looking at the album. "Here she is with her gray stripedy cat," he said.

"His name was Mittens. He had four white paws, see? She loved him nearly as much as she did Uncle Sandy. He got killed by a car and she buried him and put up a tombstone and planted forget-me-nots on his grave. She was very sad when she talked about Mittens."

"Your mama was sad a lot," Greg said pityingly.

"Yes. I guess she didn't have much fun after she left the gingerbread house. But it was great there! Except, of course, when Mittens died. Oh, I do hope we can find it!"

"Here's a picture of the school," Ronny said. "But even with my magnifying glass I can't see the name on the front. It's just a big old brick school. Looks like a million other old-fashioned schools."

"But," Greg pointed out, "it seems to be kind of up high, see? With steps going up to it on some banks of grass or something—not on a level place like our school. So, maybe if we saw one like that anywhere—"

"That's not grass; it's ivy," Dad told them. "So look for a school that has banks of ivy in front. Probably an old school, because it takes a long time for ivy to cover a bank. And this isn't modern school architecture."

"And it'll be a school that begins with a B," Evie said, "because of her cheerleader sweater."

"The phone book again," Dad said to Ronny. "My dear Holmes, why don't you look up Atlanta's city high schools?"

"You don't even need the magnifying glass for that," Greg said.

"Elementary," Ronny muttered, turning the pages.

"No, not an elementary school; a high school—get it?" Greg said, and ducked when Ronny made a pass at him. "Ha. Can't you take a joke?"

"Hey," Ronny said, ignoring Greg's levity. "Look! There are only two high schools that begin with a B.

Brown and Bass. Dad, do you know where they are?"

"I think I can tell by the addresses. Let's see—Bass must be in the Little Five Points area. That's where they're building the new freeway to Stone Mountain, through that area. And Brown—Brown is the high school in the old section of West End. Not far from here."

"It figures!" Ronny exclaimed excitedly. "The house has gotta be somewhere in West End. Because, you know, Evie, those Jowers kids sort of recognized it— and if it's some place they know, around here, the school would have to be, too—"

"We've gotta go look at that school and see if it looks at all like this picture," Evie agreed. "And then look around that neighborhood for gingerbread houses."

"Is it okay for them to explore West End?" Mama asked Dad.

"Why not?" Dad shrugged. "Three of them ought to be safe enough, if they stay together. You guys stay together, understand?" Ronny knew Dad liked for them to practice being self-reliant.

"We'll be careful," he promised. "We'll take Froman. He's a police dog. Well, about a quarter police, any-how. I think. He'll sic anybody I tell him to sic."

"So don't tell him to," Dad advised. "That could get you in real trouble."

"But if somebody jumped on us, it would be okay to let Froman do whatever he wanted to, wouldn't it? And he would want to sic 'em even if we didn't tell him to, if they bothered us."

"Use your own judgment, men," Dad said. "I have every confidence in you and Froman. Just be home at mealtimes."

"Oh, you can count on us for that," Greg said earnestly. "Detective work makes you very hungry. And police dogs have to eat regular or they can't smell out criminals."

"Let's don't go smelling out any criminals," Dad said. "Just Evie's grandmother and uncle."

Next morning, as soon as she had called up the hospital and learned that Mrs. Lewis was still unconscious, Mama offered to drive them by Brown High School to compare it with the picture. She was going to the grocery store afterward, and it wasn't much out of the way.

"Well, there it is," she said as they turned the corner.

"No luck," Evie said disappointedly. "It doesn't have a high bank at all. So this wasn't the high school my mother and Uncle Sandy went to."

"Tough," Greg said.

"No!" Ronny thought it might be good luck after all. "Don't you see, my dear Watson? This narrows it down to the other school that begins with a B."

"Quite so, Holmes. Mama, would you drive us to see that other school?"

"Not this morning—I've got too much to do. Your dad said last night that Bass High School is way over in Little Five Points. But why don't you telephone and ask if it's up on a high bank?"

"Who'd we phone?"

"The school—no, probably nobody would be there during vacation. Call the city Board of Education— somebody there in the office might know."

The boys rushed for the telephone as soon as they got back from the grocery store, hurriedly grabbing a sack of groceries apiece to carry into the kitchen.

Mattie was out in the yard with Joy in her arms. "Takin' her for a little walk," she explained when Evie stopped to kiss the baby.

"She loves to go for walks," Evie said happily. "Thanks, Mattie."

"Where the boys runnin' to so fast?"

"They're telephoning to find out about a high school."

Mattie chuckled. "They ain't passed grammar school yet."

Evie didn't wait to explain. She was eager to know about Bass, too. But Ronny was hanging up the receiver, shaking his head.

"That old Board of Education is pretty dumb," he told her. "The lady in their office says she's never seen Bass School and she doesn't have any idea what it looks like. She went to Russell High, she said. I asked her didn't they even have a picture of it, and she said no. Its address is Euclid Avenue, she says, if we want to go and see it."

"Mama'll have to take us," Greg said. "Or else we can go on the bus."

"You know Mama never would let us go through town on the bus if we have to transfer," Ronny said. "And that would sure be a transfer."

"Well, maybe she'll take us. Now let's call Dad and see if he found out about the telephone number."

"It'll just be another false lead," Ronny grumbled, and he was right. All Dad could find out was that the 522 exchange included the downtown area and most of the close-in residential districts.

Then Ronny had another idea. "But, Dad—could it be the exchange for the section of town where Bass

High School is? Euclid Avenue? Is that close enough in?"

"Look it up, my dear Holmes," Dad advised. "You know I don't do any detective work for you guys that you can do yourself. This time was an exception."

"Thanks," Ronny said. "I'll look it up, Dad."

Greg had already found it. "It is!" he shouted. "The phone number for Bass High is 522–1774."

"That means it might be the neighborhood where Evie's mother went to school!"

"What it means," Evie said, "is that now we've got to explore both places—West End and Little Five Points. Because those Jowers kids looked like they'd seen the house, and that would've been in West End, remember?"

"It's gotta be Little Five Points," Ronny insisted. "West End's phone exchange number is 344. That's ours, see? And the school doesn't look right."

"But Bim and Toby knew something about that gingerbread house. They'd hardly have gone over to Little Five Points," Evie said stubbornly.

"Hey, Ron, can Watson have an idea?" Greg asked.

"Sure—you got one?"

"Why don't we advertise in the paper for Evie's grandmother? Like in the personal column? 'Anybody that saw a white dog that bit a kid last Thursday on the corner of Gordon and Beecher please call—' "

"Hey, that's a great idea," Evie said, complimenting him, and Greg ducked his head, pleased. " 'Any lady that has a daughter named Christina Elizabeth she hasn't seen for fourteen years please call—what's your number?—344-8655—if she wants to see her two granddaughters.' Wonder how much it would cost to put that in?"

"We could find out," Ronny said. "Right after lunch. The West End paper—*The Weekly Star*—is right over on Gordon Street. We can walk over there easy. And I've got a good bit of money in my bank. You have too, Greg. And Mama would even advance allowances for a thing like this."

"Okay," Greg said. "Quite so, I mean, my dear Holmes. It's a real good idea, huh, Ron?"

"It really is," Ronny said generously. "And then if the ad in *The Star* doesn't bring any answers in, maybe we could put it in a paper in Little Five Points, if there is one. Or in the big Atlanta papers—in case Evie's grandmother moved to some other part of town."

"You don't suppose she moved out of town, do you?" Evie said anxiously. "No, I guess not—Mother must have known she was still here or she wouldn't have come back to Atlanta. And I don't think she'd have moved to some other part of town, either. The gingerbread house was her family home. She wouldn't have left it. I'll go fix up the ad."

"And that's another point," Ronny said. "Is this the right section of town to look for your mother's old home in, because she would have come back to live close to it—or is it the wrong section to look for it in, because she wouldn't have wanted her mother to see her accidentally, like at the shopping center?"

"It's a tossup," Greg said seriously. "I mean, quite so, my dear Holmes."

After lunch, as soon as Joy went to sleep, the three walked over to the community newspaper office. Froman came too. Ronny, with Evie and Greg right behind him, was placing the ad. A sympathetic young woman, whose name on the desk sign was Miss Carson, helped him. She glanced at Evie with interest as he explained her problem. "Maybe we can get an answer," Miss Carson said. "That would be good, wouldn't it?"

A working file of the weekly paper for the past year lay open on the counter. Evie said to Greg, "Let's see if there are any ads sort of like this, in their 'Personals.'" Idly she turned the pages, and then she came to the want ad section of several weeks back.

"Hey! Look at this!" She pointed to a display ad

down in the corner of the page that had caught her eye.

"Hey—Ronny!" Greg grabbed at Ronny. "Look at this!"

Ronny finished putting the change in his pocket. "Now what?" he said. "My dear Watson—"

Then he saw the ad, and leaned across Evie to see it better. "It can't be—" He was just as excited as Greg and Evie.

"What do you make of *that*, my dear Holmes?" Greg said triumphantly.

# The Boxwood House
# and the Man Upstairs

It was a real estate company's ad, showing the pictures of several houses for sale.

"It is!" Evie said, catching her breath. "Ron, quit breathing down my neck. It's the house! Look at the door—and the gingerbread. And the way the porch goes all around the house. And the steps like she sat on. And the pillars. Only I don't see the house number on that front one."

"That was a long time ago, that it had a number on that post," Greg pointed out. "It could have fallen off. And the print's not too clear, anyhow."

"But that looks like boxwood in front," Ronny said. "You said it had boxwood in the yard."

"This picture doesn't show the trees," Evie said.

"And the end is hidden where the rose vine was. And —if it's for sale—my grandmother might not still be there."

"But she might," Miss Carson offered. "Often people put up houses for sale while they're still living in them."

"I don't think my grandmother would want to sell it. She—she might have died? But no—I'm sure Mother came back here because she wanted to be near her mother even if she didn't let her know it. Oh, it would be awful if—if my grandmother has died since—and we'd never get to see her—"

"That ad's been running a long time," Miss Carson said, to comfort her. "So whoever owned the house probably didn't die recently."

Evie smiled, hopefully, then.

"Look at the address!" Ronny wrote it down in his notebook. "1560 Boxwood Avenue."

"It's not the right number—not 250." Greg frowned. "I sure am sorry, Evie. I thought we had it."

"I won't give up yet," Evie said. "Sometimes they change house numbers. They did once when we lived in Verde. They changed the name of the street from 31st to Fremont, and changed all the house numbers."

"Well, we'll go and look at it, and if it seems like the right house, Dad can probably find out if the house numbers were ever changed. Down at the city hall or somewhere."

"He'll tell us to find out," Greg prophesied.

Miss Carson, who had been showing a lively interest in their quest, said, "Do you want to see that house? Because it might be her grandmother's? It's not far from here. Boxwood Avenue runs off Olympia, and Olympia curves around from Beecher."

"Let's go!" Ronny said. "I know where Olympia is. Ted used to live there."

It wasn't easy, to hurry and yet wait for Evie without letting her notice they were waiting for her. And a thunderstorm was coming up. Ronny kept looking apprehensively at the sky, which was getting darker and darker. One of Mama's rules was that they should always come home when a storm seemed to be brewing. Still, as Dad said, they had to use their own judgment, and anybody's judgment could be wrong when it came to the weather. Even the weatherman's—he was wrong fairly often. So maybe the storm would blow over—or they could get to Boxwood Avenue and on home before it broke.

They felt the first drops of rain just as they saw the street sign that said *Boxwood Avenue*.

"Maybe it'll just be a shower," Greg said, turning his

shoulder to a gust of wind that seemed about to blow his shirt off. "What a funny old street, with big yards and big houses, but—it used to be a nice street, and then something happened to it."

Ronny was thinking. What happened was that the nice people moved away. Maybe that's why whoever owns the house now is trying to sell it. I hope Evie's grandmother doesn't still live around here. Half the houses don't seem to have anybody at all living in them.

"This number is 1544," Evie said. "So 1560 is a few more houses down the block." They hurried, Froman cavorting ahead of them, watering a tree now and then. The yards were large and the number they wanted was nearly at the end of the block.

"There it is!"

They stood in front of the house and looked. "No trees," Evie said slowly. "So we can't tell if there were oaks and chinaberries or not."

"They were cut down," Ronny said. "Look, there are some big stumps."

"No rose vine—"

"It probably died, in all that time. The house looks empty. Let's walk around to the back."

Greg said, "Look at all the cars in the back yard."

"They're not all old ones, either," Ronny pointed out. "Not just junked ones. There're three pretty good second-hand cars. A Mustang and a Dart—and two or three Falcons and Chevys in the two garages or barns or whatever those open sheds are. Somebody must live here."

"Do we dare ring the doorbell?"

"I dare," Evie said firmly. "Come on."

They circled back around the shabby house, and Evie looked for a rose-vine root at both sides of the porch, but she found nothing but weeds and tin cans. The front steps looked just like the ones the girl in the snapshot was sitting on with her gray-striped cat in her arms, except for the peeling paint. The boards of the porch were rotten in places; they stepped carefully, but once Evie's crutch nearly went through.

"There's the stained glass on both sides of the door," Ronny said. "What's left of it." He peered in. "The hall looks empty. Dark, too."

"But the glass isn't in diamond-shaped panes." Evie frowned. "These are more squared off."

"That's a lot of years. Could have been replaced?"

"I don't know. This looks like it's been here forever. Well, let's ring, anyhow, and see if anybody lives here."

They pushed the bell, but could hear no ring. "I

know—the electricity's been turned off!" Ronny said. "Let's knock. Real hard." He beat on the door, but nobody answered. Through the broken panes they could hear the knocking echoed.

Just then the storm broke in a fury of wind and gusts of rain that swept across the old porch. The once-white, lacy, wooden gingerbread around the top of it creaked, and a section fell with a crash.

"We better get inside," Greg said. "If the door's unlocked."

"We aren't allowed to go in empty houses," Ronny reminded him.

"But this one probably isn't empty," Greg argued. "We don't know whether it is or not, till we go in. Somebody must live here, to have all those cars."

"Well, technically you might be right," Ronny admitted. "But I don't think we're allowed to go in strange houses whether anybody lives in them or not."

"We aren't allowed to be out in thunderstorms either," Greg said. There was a flash of lightning and a big clap of thunder sounded so close they jumped, and Evie screamed. She pushed the door and it opened. At the next flash of lightning they jumped again, and somehow they seemed to have jumped inside. Froman too, shaking his rain on everybody.

They stood in a high-ceilinged, desolate hall. Brownish wallpaper with stains on its brownish flowers was peeling off the walls.

"There's a staircase," Evie said slowly. "And it does have a landing with a stained-glass window, like Mother used to play on."

"I don't see how anybody can be living here," Greg said, "even if it's where they do keep their cars. No electricity—"

"They might have a pad upstairs," Evie suggested.

"I was just about to observe," Ronny said reprovingly, in his Sherlock voice, "that someone is obviously living upstairs."

"How do you deduce that, my dear Holmes?" Greg said amiably.

"It is simplicity itself," Ronny told him. "Observe the stairs. There is dust on them, but it has been walked on. We can't even take casts of the footprints, because they are all over each other. Somebody has been going up and down—"

"We couldn't take casts of the footprints anyhow," Greg said practically, "because we don't know how."

"It's getting darker," Evie said nervously. "We'd better look for the fireplace with the mirror and then go."

Suddenly Greg yelled, "I see him! He's upstairs now! He was looking down over the banister. It was a

man—but I couldn't see him very well. And he's gone now—"

"Run!" Ronny said, and he and Greg made a break for the front door. But Evie—though she was pale around the mouth—said, "I'm not going till I see if that fireplace with the mirror over it is in the front room. Anyhow, he's not coming down the stairs. He's staying up there. He must not want anybody to see him." Froman stood by her, barking furiously.

"That's right." Ronny came back to where she was

standing, and Greg followed. "If he hasn't got any right to be in here, he wouldn't want us to be able to identify him in the police lineup. So he wouldn't want us to see him. He's gotta be doing something wrong. Hold Froman, Greg—we don't want him going after criminals. He might get hurt."

"So let's look in the front room," Evie said. "It would probably be the living room." She put her hand on the knob of the closed door, and shut her eyes for a minute as if she were praying. But Ronny couldn't tell whether she was praying for it to be the right house— or for it not to be.

The door stuck a little. Greg, holding Froman by the collar, kept on looking over his shoulder at the staircase, as if he didn't exactly trust the man upstairs to stay there, lineup or not. Froman kept on barking.

It was the right kind of room, Ronny saw—big and high-ceilinged and old fashioned.

"But it's not the right kind of fireplace," Evie said dejectedly.

"But look!" Ronny said to her. Then he remembered. "I mean, I deduce, Miss Morstan, that it's been rebuilt to look like a modern fireplace that burns logs. Observe, my dear Watson. You can see where it used to have a high mantel like that, and they took it down and papered over it and fixed the mantel without the mirror. So"—he became Ronny again—"it could've been the right one."

"We'll never know," Evie said disconsolately. "There are so many ways it might have been the right house —but no way to really know whether it is or isn't."

"Anyhow, your grandmother doesn't live here now," Ronny said, "thank goodness. So we'll just concentrate on finding her, instead of the house." ·

"But how?"

"I have my methods, Miss Morstan. You will observe—"

"Let's go home," Greg said, interrupting, "before that man upstairs gets tired of observing three kids poking around down here, and chases us."

"Aw, he doesn't want us to see him," Ronny said confidently. "But it's nearly suppertime. Let's go."

They shut the heavy front door carefully behind them. Then Ronny had another idea. "Wait a minute," he said. "Lucky I've got my notebook. I'm going to take down all the tag numbers on those old cars. There must be some place where they know who owns a car by the tag. Maybe Dad could find out—or tell us how to. Then if it happened to be somebody who knows about who used to own this house—"

The rain had stopped. Evie and Greg and Froman

waited while he wrote down the license-tag numbers of the cars. "But," Ronny said when he finished, "they're not Georgia tags, my dear Watson. That makes our task harder. Maybe impossible. They're all from other states. Like Arizona and California and Nevada."

"Like they're stolen cars," Greg said.

"My dear Watson, it is a capital mistake to theorize before one has data. If the cars were stolen cars, the tags would have been changed to Georgia tags, to make them not so easy to see in Atlanta where there are so many Georgia tags."

"We'll have to ask Dad how to find out about the owners, then," Greg said.

"It'd be easier," Evie said gloomily, as if she didn't think anything they could possibly do would help, "to ask the real estate company who owns the house. And we could ask them if they rented it to that man who was upstairs. Not that it matters—of course my grandmother must have sold it ages ago—if it was the right house to begin with. I never thought she'd sell it, though. It'd kill Mother to know that."

"We'll try the real estate company, of course," Ronny said. "But let's get home now, before Mama has a conniption."

"Hey!" Greg said. "I—I saw somebody—around the corner of that shed."

Froman growled and then barked.

"I did too!" Evie said. "And I saw who it was! It was Bim Jowers."

# The Hospital Clue

Bim! We saw you!" Ronny shouted.

"Aw, let him go," Evie said. "He wouldn't tell us anything even if he knew it."

"And besides, we're due home for supper," Greg said.

"Okay. But that's why he recognized the picture of your grandmother's house, Evie. He'd been here."

"Well, maybe this one wasn't my grandmother's house."

Evie sounded discouraged; so Ronny told her his plan for tomorrow. "We'll try to get Mama to take us to see Bass High School, and if it's the right one, then maybe she'll drive around that section and let us look for gingerbread houses."

His plan had to be changed, though. But he didn't mind, because the new events turned out to be much more exciting. When they got home, Mama met them at the door, with news.

"Hurry and let's get supper, children," she said. "The hospital called, and Evie's mother seems to be getting better—at least she's stirring and getting restless, and they think she may be coming out of the coma. And they think it might help if Evie went and spoke to her. So after supper I'm going to take Evie to the hospital."

"Can we go too?" Greg said.

"I suppose you could ride over there with us. But you'll have to stay in the car—or in the hospital's waiting room."

"Can Froman go too?"

"Why not?" Mama knew when she was licked. "If you stay in the car with him."

"How about Joy?" Evie asked. "Wouldn't it help Mother to see Joy too?"

"Well, if she recognizes you, we'll take Joy next time. You mustn't expect too much, you know. She wasn't really conscious yet. It was just that her condition had changed from being in a coma. I think that means she was lying perfectly still before—and now she's moving about. So it's hopeful—she might be coming out of it."

"Thanks, Mrs. Jameson. But if we both go, who'll take care of Joy? Mattie's off."

"Mattie is baby-sitting for us tonight. She wanted to, when she heard, because she wants you to get to see your mother."

"And Dad will be here," Greg said, "in case Mattie has a heart attack or drops dead or anything. So Joy will be okay."

"I'll go and tell Mattie thank you," Evie said soberly.

On the way to the hospital she sat quietly beside Mama in the front seat, while the boys roughhoused with Froman in back. They hadn't dressed up, but Evie had put on a neat skirt and blouse instead of her usual shorts and shirt. She even wore socks, Ronny noticed. Going to see somebody in a hospital sure changed people. Evie acted almost grown-up. Greg whispered to Ronny, "Evie's scared. She's holding her hands so tight."

"Try to relax, Evie," Mama said kindly. "They're doing everything they can for her—and that's a lot, these days. Medical science does perform miracles. Try not to worry."

"I just hope she can talk to me. Because she

wouldn't want Joy and me to be separated. She'd tell me how to find my grandmother, if she knew there was any danger of that."

It seemed like hours, to Ronny, before his mother and Evie came back. Froman even went to sleep. Greg was yawning, but Ronny was too excited to be sleepy. What would Evie's mother say, if she could talk at all?

"Well, it's encouraging," Mama told them as she and Evie got back in the car. "Mrs. Lewis wasn't fully conscious, of course, and yet she seemed to know Evie was there."

"She must be going to die," Evie said troubledly. "She called me Evelyn. Mrs. Jameson, she never called me Evelyn. She always called me Evie."

"I don't think that means she's worse, necessarily," Mama said comfortingly. "Who can tell what's going through someone's confused mind, in a state like hers? After all, it is your name."

"Yes'm."

"What else did she say?" Ronny asked.

"Not much," Evie answered. "She kept her eyes shut, but she did seem to know I was there. She just muttered things we couldn't understand. About all I could get was my name, and just a word or two besides. But I think she was trying to tell me about the key to the trunk. Maybe it's got something real important in it, that she wants me to know about, now that she can't be with me and Joy."

"What did she say about it?"

"All I could make out was something that sounded like 'key—trunk—look under the frog—' It doesn't make sense, of course. We didn't have any frog statuettes or anything like that."

"Did Joy have a toy frog?" Greg asked. "Once I saw a movie where the important papers were sewed up in a stuffed doll."

"Yes! Come to think about it, Joy had a real cute stuffed frog. But she said 'under the frog,' I think—not 'in' it. And once I had a frog bank, but I don't remember where it is, if we brought it with us when we moved. Mother threw away a lot of stuff. We'll go back to the house tomorrow and look for it, though."

"And if you don't find it," Mama said, "of course we can get a locksmith to open the trunk."

"I guess she'd want me to, now," Evie said hesitantly. "But she did tell me not to ever bother it."

"Things change," Mama said. "I think she'd want you to, as things are. I think that's what she meant—what she was trying to tell you."

"'Course she did, if she told you where the key is," Ronny said. "We'll help you find that frog. Maybe there's an old cement one in the back yard. I saw a frog in a yard once, with water coming out of its mouth into a pool."

"I don't think so," Evie said. "But there's an old shed back there with all sorts of junk in it. I was scared to go plundering, because there might be rats or snakes or black widows or something, Mother said. But maybe she found a cement frog in there."

"We'll look."

They could hardly wait for morning. Evie wanted to call the hospital first, of course, before they did anything. But when Mama called, after breakfast, the report was that Mrs. Lewis's condition was unchanged. Mama insisted on speaking to the floor nurse, and was told that Mrs. Lewis had a restless night but now seemed to be sinking back into unconsciousness. The doctor hadn't seen her yet.

"Poor Mother," Evie said. "I wish—I wish I could do something for her."

"Well," Ronny said practically, "it would probably make you feel better if you looked for the key under the frog. That was what she wanted you to do."

"Yes." Evie brightened up a bit. "She did. We'll go as soon as I feed Joy and put her to sleep." When Ronny looked impatient, she added, "Well, she'd want me to take care of Joy, too."

Mama was going off to a meeting and luncheon, but she said it was okay for them to go, just so they were back by lunchtime. The phone rang just as Evie was settling Joy into her basket, and woke her. She whimpered. Evie murmured to the baby and patted her, and she snuggled down with a final sniffle. Ronny came to the door and whispered so as not to wake Joy again. "It's for you."

"Me? Nobody would be calling me." Evie whispered too. She came out into the hall and closed the door.

"It's Aunt Riah," Ronny said with excitement. "Something must have happened."

"Honey," Aunt Riah said, "they's a man been foolin' 'round yo' yard. He drive a car and park it in yo' back yard. I see him over there two or three times in a car, but them cottonwoods so thick I can't see too good what he doin'."

"Did he get in the house, Aunt Riah?"

Ronny and Greg had their heads close to Evie's, listening in.

"No, I don' think so. I reckon he 'fraid the polices get him if he break in any house, and you got it locked up right good. Anyhow, I ain' seen no light in it nights. But he do hang 'round the yard a right smart. I see him come and go, and once they was another man with him. Sometimes them Jowers boys are 'round there, too."

"Is he there now?"

"No. He was there early this mornin' but he went off awhile ago."

"We're coming right over. Thanks for letting us know, Aunt Riah. We'll see you." Evie hung up and said, "Let's hurry, while he's not there."

"Good-by, Mattie," Ronny said. "We'll be back for lunch. Let's have hot dogs, huh? Since Mama won't be here. Mama hates hot dogs for lunch," he confided to Evie, "except at cookouts. Or when we're traveling and she doesn't want to spend the money for a regular restaurant."

"You'll listen out for Joy, please, Mattie?" Evie asked.

"I sho will. I got nothin' to do this mornin' but clean the kitchen and listen out for Joy."

"Thanks, Mattie."

Aunt Riah was in her front yard, pulling weeds from around her herbs. The herbs looked like weeds, too, to Ronny—he wondered how she knew the difference. There was one that looked just like dog fennel—and smelled like it, too. He had snitched a leaf and smelled it, when she wasn't looking.

"Hey, isn't this a weed, Aunt Riah?" he asked.

"Honey, a weed is a plant you don' want. I wants that one, so it ain' no weed. Some folks might think it a weed, but it make a mighty fine poultice for a sick dog do he get snake-bit."

"Hey, will you make one for Froman if he gets sick, Aunt Riah?"

"I might, do you ask me polite."

"You mean 'Please'?" Greg said. "I will."

Aunt Riah smiled, and they almost saw her gums, but not quite enough to tell if they were really blue or not.

Evie said, "Let's go on in the house and see if we can find that frog. We just stopped by to say hello, Aunt Riah. We've got to find the key to my mother's trunk." She told the old woman about the visit to the hospital.

"You go ahead, Evie honey. I go inside and whip up a spell that says you find the key. I think I got some powdered frog skin somewheres—and senna opens up things, so it ought to help open that trunk—"

"You sure know a lot, Aunt Riah," Greg said respectfully. "And I sure do appreciate that buckeye you gave me. It's so shiny and brown, like a big hard polished nut. I carry it all the time."

"Buckeye might be good to use for the spell, too, for

luck," Aunt Riah said. "I reckon powdered buckeye would do it."

"The man hasn't come back, has he, Aunt Riah?" Evie asked.

"No, honey. Coast is clear."

Evie opened the front door with her key. Everything seemed in order, until Greg happened to glance out the kitchen window. "Hey!" he said. "Whoever he is, he's got two cars. He's parked them in your back yard, Evie."

"I bet it's those Jowers kids," Evie said vindictively. "They're always messing around with old cars, souping them up for drag races and all like that. They've got no business putting them in our yard, though, even if we aren't here right now."

"What's the matter with their own yard?" Ronny said.

"Aw, it's full of junk. Old junk cars mostly. But cans and bottles and stuff too."

"Well—let's look for the frog. Where did Joy have her toy frog?"

"It might be in the back bedroom someplace. I don't think I took any of her toys last time we were here— we had too many clothes to carry. We'll take her the frog this time." Evie led the way.

"Here it is!" Greg picked the toy up. "But there's no key on the shelf under it."

Evie took it from him and felt all over it carefully. "No key inside it, either," she said, disappointed. "It's so soft, you see, we could feel a thing like that, if it were there."

Ronny felt it too, and then Greg. "No, there sure isn't any key in it."

"Well, where did you keep your frog bank?" Ronny asked.

"Let's see—I don't believe I've thought of that frog bank since we moved. There are some boxes in the closet that Mother hadn't unpacked, stuff we didn't need right at first. It might be in there."

They dumped everything out of the boxes, but the frog wasn't among the miscellany. Evie put it all back, while the boys looked all over the house for pictures of frogs or statuettes or anything that might be green and hopped. Evie said, "Mother unpacked some stuff and put it on the closet shelves. Let's stand on a chair and look up there."

Ronny climbed up and looked. "Hey—here's your frog bank, Evie!"

"Anything under it?"

"Not a thing." He was disappointed too. He shook

it, handing it down to her. "But it does have something inside it. Maybe the key?"

"Just my Kennedy half dollar," Evie said. "But I'm glad that wasn't lost. Mother gave it to me."

They went into her mother's bedroom and looked at the locked trunk. It was a substantial one, with a set-in lock that would be hard to pry open. "It could be broken into, I guess," Ronny said, "if somebody like Dad or a locksmith tried hard. But I don't believe we kids could do it."

"I'd rather not break it if I can help it," Evie said slowly. "Though of course we might have to get somebody to do it. But somehow I don't like breaking into anybody's secret place. Everybody ought to have a secret place, where nobody else can see into it, ever. It doesn't even seem right that after you die other people can look at your secret places. If Mother had things in here she didn't want anybody but her to see —then I oughtn't to—"

"Your mother isn't going to die," Ronny said, though he didn't feel too sure. "And anyhow, you're forgetting. She was trying to tell you where the key is. So she wants you to get into the trunk."

"That's right," Evie said. "I guess she does want me to. But I'd rather use the key than break the lock."

"So let's go look for that cement frog that might be in the yard."

The shed had plenty of junk in it, and most of it looked absolutely worthless. Empty boxes and broken furniture and chipped china and old jars and rusty tools. There were old garden things, too, flower pots and tools and dusty bowls and baskets, though it would have been years since any lady had arranged flowers here for a flower show, like Mama sometimes did. But in all the clutter there were no cement frogs from garden pools. One live toad-frog leaped from a corner and scared them. "Reckon he's trying to tell us something?" Ronny said. But the toad hopped away before Greg could see where it had been sitting, to look for a key there.

"Ha," Ronnie scoffed. "He sat there only about a minute."

"I was doing that for a joke," Greg explained. "I thought you all would think it was funny."

"I did," Evie said consolingly. "Well, I guess we'd better go clean up—we're getting pretty dirty out here. And I don't believe we'll ever find the key."

Aunt Riah, when they went back by her house on the way home, assured them that they would. "But it might take a little time for this spell to work," she said. "Buckeyes grows slow. Don' you give up, Evie honey. You gon' get that trunk open, sooner or later."

Like when Dad gets a locksmith to open it, Ronny thought. But of course it would be more fun to find the frog. And we always have to wait till Dad gets the time, before he can do anything, and he's so busy all the time. Mama too. When I grow up I'm going to find a job that doesn't have so much work to it. And my wife's not going to belong to so many clubs.

Then he thought, No—that's not fair. They take us places pretty often, and play games and all with us. They're real good parents, actually. They just make us do things on our own so we'll be independent, I reckon, and self-reliant. At least, that's what Dad told Mama that time.

Evie asked Aunt Riah to let them know any new developments, like if the strange man should break into the house; and they started home. Evie had thought this was a good time to take the painting her mother had made of the house; so Ronny and Greg were carrying it between them. She carried Joy's frog and a few more of the baby's toys, and her own frog bank with her Kennedy half dollar in it.

Just as they reached their own sidewalk, Ronny said, "Hey, Evie—this picture's not in the frame too good. In fact, I think the frame may be breaking up."

Greg grabbed at it, but the glass was already falling out of the frame, which was coming apart at two of its corners. It had no backing except cardboard which had been stuck into the frame with thumb tacks.

"Maybe we can put it together again," Ronny said. "We got a tool box last Christmas. Real tools."

"Hey," Greg said. "There's your mama's initials, Evie! Right there at the right hand bottom corner where she signed it, see? They were hidden under the edge of the frame until it came off."

"Where?" Evie said, excited. Then she sighed. "Oh, dear, I thought we had something at last. But she just signed her first two initials. It's only *C. E.* for Christina Elizabeth—no last name. She was just a kid when she painted it, you know."

"Sorry, Evie." Ronny carefully carried the water color into the house, while Greg brought the glass and pieces of frame.

"Well, let's see if Mattie cooked the hot dogs," Greg said philosophically.

"I ought to play with Joy awhile," Evie said. "She likes to be played with. So I'll hold her till lunch is ready. You know Mattie wasn't about to cook those hot dogs till we showed up."

The hot dogs were good, but after Ronny had another idea they could hardly wait to finish them.

"Hey," he said, "I've been wondering, Evie, about that medal of your mother's that you're wearing. Looks like we'd be able to trace who won it, if we asked the U. D. C. They're bound to have records that ought to keep up with things like that, or else what are they in business for? It's worth a try."

"You're right," Evie said, swallowing her milk fast. "I'll get the telephone book."

"It's let us down again," Greg grumbled, when they couldn't find any listing for U. D. C. "That old phone company never has anything we want in their old book."

"Well," Ronny said, "why don't we go back to *The Star* office, and see if that nice lady there, Miss Carson, knows where the U. D. C. meets? I remember they have a page with all kinds of stuff specially for ladies to read, like about Mama's garden club and flower shows and all, and sometimes it has heads like 'Club News' and 'Meetings.' Maybe it would tell about the U. D. C. meeting, or who's president of it, or something that'd help."

"Good idea," Evie said approvingly.

"Quite so, my dear Holmes," Greg said.

Miss Carson at *The Star* was sympathetic when they told her they couldn't be sure whether the house was the right one or not, but they hoped not. She wrote down the number of the real estate company for them. She hadn't had any inquiries about the ad they had placed.

"We didn't get any calls either, yet," Ronny told her.

"Maybe you should put the ad in the Atlanta papers," Miss Carson suggested. "The grandmother might have moved—even if she once lived in West End."

"I guess so."

When Ronny explained their new idea, Miss Carson let them look through the recent files of the paper for "Club News" on the Women's Pages of each issue, trying to find a mention of the United Daughters of the Confederacy.

Greg was about to get discouraged, searching for something as elusive as that, but Ronny and Evie persevered. " 'If at first you don't succeed,' " Evie quoted, " 'try, try again.' That's what the proverb says."

"But it doesn't say anything about the sixth and seventh and eighth times," Greg pointed out. "It just says 'if at first.' What about if at tenth you don't succeed?"

"I'm not giving up," Evie said. "If you needed to find out as bad as I do, Greg Jameson, you wouldn't either. It's just a game to you and Ron. But I've just got to find my grandmother, or—or Joy and I—might not have anybody—of our own—"

"Don't cry," Greg begged her. "I didn't mean—"

"Hey!" Ronny said. "Here it is! We've got it at last. Here's a story about the U. D. C. records being kept at Rhodes Memorial Hall, wherever that is."

"It's a fine old building at Rhodes Center," Miss Carson told him. "Long ago it was the Rhodes family's home. Then the State Archives and History Department was there; but now they've moved to a new building."

"So where's Rhodes Center?"

Miss Carson told them which bus to take to get

there. "It's where Peachtree and West Peachtree run together," she said. "Ask the bus driver—he'll point out the building to you."

"Thanks, Miss Carson," Evie said gratefully. "If we find out my mother's born name from the U. D. C., it'll fix everything for me and Joy."

"Well, maybe not everything," Miss Carson said gently. "You'll still have to find your grandmother. I surely hope it helps, though."

Greg was already at the door, and Ronny was waiting politely to tell Miss Carson thanks and good-by, idly reading cutlines under other pictures on the Women's Page.

Then he saw it.

He closed the newspaper file deliberately, so that Evie would be mystified. "Miss Morstan," he said, "you know my methods. I have discovered where the missing key to the trunk is."

# The Man with
# the Stolen Cars

Good-by, Miss Carson," Evie said hurriedly. "Come on, then, Ron!"

"Thanks, Miss Carson," Ronny said, not hurrying, keeping Evie in suspense on purpose.

"Good luck, kids," Miss Carson smiled. Greg waved from the door.

When they were outside, Evie said, "Tell us. Hurry."

"No," Ronny said. "If I tell you now, you'll want to go right back there and open the trunk. And then we won't have time to go to Rhodes Center and trace the medal this afternoon. So let's go to the U. D. C. first, and afterward, if there's time, we'll get the key and open the trunk. You see, we don't know what clues the trunk will give us—it might not tell us anything at all about who your grandmother was. But if we can find out who won the medal, we're bound to have your mother's born name. So that's more important right now than the trunk."

"I guess you're right," Evie admitted. "Though Mother did seem to want me to open the trunk. But it might have been something else in there—not about my grandmother—that she wanted me to get."

"Like money," Greg said. "She might be worrying about how you and Joy are going to get along, and if she had any money hidden in there she would want you to get it out and use it."

"Yes," Evie said, getting excited now. "And that would explain—if she does have money there—what it was Finch was always wanting her to give him, that she wouldn't. But—no, I don't think she could have had any money, or we wouldn't have been so hard up. She'd've used some of it. I think she said all she had was that last unemployment check of Finch's. But she did have something she didn't want him to have. And it's probably in the trunk. Ron, are you sure you know where the key is? I wish you'd tell me!"

"Well, I might be mistaken," Ronny said. "So I don't want to tell you yet. It's just a guess, actually. I mean not really a scientific deduction. If I don't tell you yet, maybe you won't be so disappointed if I'm not right as you would be if you were believing it too. Anyhow, we've agreed to try the U. D. C. first—right?"

"You've agreed all by yourself," Greg said glumly. "Evie and I didn't get a vote."

"I think he's probably right, Greg," Evie said, "even though I know he's being mysterious just to bug us."

"Okay," Greg said. "Have we got enough money for bus fare?"

"I brought my allowance," Ronny said. "That'll get us there and back. I was going to get Froman a new collar, but he won't mind waiting for that."

"Froman wouldn't mind going naked, without any collar at all," Greg said certainly.

"He has to wear his tag."

"Hey, there's Mama! I wasn't expecting to see her. She's blowing the horn at us."

It was the station wagon, and the three hurried to get in.

"Hey, Mama," Ronny said, "do you have time to drive to Rhodes Center?"

"Sorry, men—no, not today. But I'm going over to Little Five Points to take some play equipment from our Community House to theirs—I volunteered just because I knew you wanted to go. I was looking for you—Mattie said you were going to the newspaper office. The other day it was Bass High School you wanted to look for. You change your objectives pretty often, Mr. Holmes."

"Well, we still want to look for the school, too, of course, Mama. But if we could get to Rhodes Center we could maybe find out the whole name of the girl who won Evie's medal from the U. D. C. That's where they have their records and stuff. Miss Carson helped us find out. She doesn't make us do all the work ourselves, like Dad does."

"If you had asked me," Mama said, laughing as she started for the Little Five Points area, "I could have told you about the U. D. C. I went to a reception at Rhodes Memorial once. It's a very historical old building. A Mrs. Baker was in charge of it then. Sometime when I have time, we'll go and see her."

"Couldn't we go by ourselves on the bus? You'll never have time. Miss Carson told us how. We were about to do that this afternoon, but now that you're going to where the school is, we might as well see it first—and maybe spot the gingerbread house! Don't you think so, Evie?"

"I guess the medal can wait, all right."

"I think so too," Greg said plaintively. "You don't ever ask me, Ron."

Mama said, "Yes, you may go on the bus tomorrow, if you can't wait for me to take you. But I usually do find time after a while, you know, Ronny. It's only that first things must come first."

Greg said, "The difference is, our first things don't exactly seem to be the same as your first things, Mama, most of the time. You even think your grocery shopping is more important than what we think is more important."

"You'd think so, too, son, if a mealtime came around and there wasn't anything to eat."

"Anyhow," Ronny said, "we're going to Rhodes Center tomorrow, one way or the other."

"Right," Evie said.

Going north and east, they were impatient to see the section of Atlanta they had never been in before; they kept asking, "Is this Little Five Points?"

"No," Mama said. "You'll recognize the center of it because it's where five streets come together, just like the Five Points in the middle of downtown Atlanta. You've seen that. But this is a big area. We won't be able to drive around enough to see it all today. We'll stop at the Community House first and deliver this stuff, and ask them where the high school is."

It turned out to be on one of the main streets leading to the center where the five streets converged.

"There it is!" Greg shouted. "It's got the high banks, all right!"

"There's more grass than ivy," Evie said slowly, "but it does look like the picture, doesn't it?" Mama slowed the car for them to get a good look.

"I'm sure that's it," Ronny said earnestly. "The grass could've outgrown the ivy since the picture was made. Now we're getting warm, Evie! And I'm glad that old house on Boxwood isn't the one."

"We're getting hot!" Evie said emphatically, with excitement. "Look at that!" She pointed to a sign over a garage a block from the school, on another of the main streets.

"Tankersley's Garage," Ronny read. "It's—"

"It's the one my mother's boyfriend's father owned," Evie said breathlessly. "Tank. The boy who gave her the cultured pearls for Christmas, and the orchid for the dance—"

"It sure is!" Greg was excited too.

"Mama," Ronny said, "can't we stop and ask at Tankersley's Garage if they used to know Christina Elizabeth? And what her last name was?"

"Why, yes," Mama agreed. She pulled in toward the mechanics' side of the garage, away from the gas tanks. The children piled out, starting to talk, all three at the same time, to the two mechanics who were working on a car.

"Wait a minute," one of them said, laughing. He

had grease on his face, but he seemed pleasant. "Talk slower. One at a time."

"You tell him, Ronny," Evie said.

"Well, it's this way," Ronny began. "Evie's mother used to know a boy named Tank, whose father owned a garage named Tankersley's in Little Five Points. We've got to find Evie's grandmother, and we thought maybe Mr. Tankersley could tell us—if he remembered—"

"Whoa," the garageman said. "I'm sorry, kids, but Mr. Tankersley died some time back. We bought this place five years ago."

"What about his son?" Evie said. "He had a boy—my mother's friend—who'd be over thirty now—"

"What became of Tank?" one mechanic asked the other. "Didn't he go to Vietnam?"

"Last I heard he was in Vietnam. It's too bad, kids, but there aren't any Tankersleys still around here, as far as I know."

"I don't suppose you ever knew a girl named Christina Elizabeth who used to go to school at Bass and was a cheerleader?" Evie asked hopelessly.

"No—we're from Roswell. We didn't go to school around here."

"Well, thanks anyway." Ronny felt the way Froman looked with his tail dragging, when he had failed to catch a car he was barking at. They got back in the car and told Mama "No luck."

"We'll drive around a bit and look for the ginger-bread house," Mama said consolingly, "but we can't stay too long. It'll take us an hour to get home, and we have to be there before time for Mattie to leave, you know."

Ronny knew they couldn't expect to find it in that short a time, and he was right. They saw lots of old houses—and some of them had gingerbread, too—but none looked like the picture.

"Well, we'll have to explore some more another day," Mama said after a while. "It's a pretty big community, you know. There are lots of other streets. Don't give up, Sherlock. The 'Tank' clue and the school clue surely point to this area."

"But the West End house the Jowers boys recognized—it might have been—" Greg just wasn't sure, yet, that the old house they had been in wasn't the one.

"It is a capital mistake, my dear Watson," Ronny repeated, "to theorize before one has all the data. What we need is more data."

"What's data? my dear Holmes."

"Facts, Greg. What we're going to find out tomorrow, when we go to the U. D. C."

"And maybe when we open the trunk," Evie said. "I wish we could open the trunk tomorrow."

"Well, why not? We can do both, with the whole day before us. It was only that this afternoon there wasn't time for both."

"Great!" Evie said, brightening. Ronny could tell that she really wanted to get into that trunk. Because she thought her mother wanted her to, he supposed.

"I guess we might open the trunk first," he said, reconsidering, to please her. "There'll still be time to go to Rhodes Center, if the clue we need isn't in the trunk."

All evening, and even next morning before they got to Evie's house, Ronny was still being mysterious about where he expected to find the key to the trunk. "It's under the frog," was all he would reveal. "Just like your mother said, Evie. That is, I hope it is. At least, I know where the frog is, and that's more than we knew the last time we were over here."

"Where?"

"Where?"

"A long shot, Watson—a very long shot."

"What's that mean?"

"Guess."

"I can't guess," Greg said. "Can you, Evie?"

"I didn't mean *to* guess," Ronny explained patiently. "I meant a long shot *is* a guess. An unlikely guess. Sherlock's long shots were usually good guesses, though. I hope mine is."

They waved to Aunt Riah, but didn't stop. She didn't holler to warn them; so they assumed the strange man wasn't around. Ronny led them straight to the back yard.

"Where are we going?" Greg asked.

"The shed is our objective, my dear Watson." Then Ronny stopped short, looking over the back yard. "Three cars this time!" He took out his notebook.

"Come on, then," Evie said.

"Wait a minute." Ronny's voice shook with excitement. "What does this tell us, my dear Watson? Miss Morstan?"

"Not a thing," Greg said cheerfully. "Except that there are three cars now and there were only two before."

"You see, Watson, but you do not observe. Look! The license tags!"

"What about them?"

"The other day," Ronny said impressively, "those two cars had Georgia tags. Now they—and the third car—have California and Nevada and Arizona tags. Like those on the cars at the house on Boxwood. And they're the same numbers! I wrote them down—remember?"

"I remember," Evie said impatiently, "but what about it? We were going to get the key from somewhere in the shed."

"Somebody—I suspect the Jowerses, but of course the strange man Aunt Riah saw is in it too—changed those numbers."

"I get it!" Greg said. "The only reason for changing license numbers is if the cars are stolen."

"Elementary, my dear Watson. Yes, that's it, Greg. I saw on TV about a stolen-car ring that operated like that, only they brought the cars from New York to Atlanta and exchanged tags with cars they stole around here. They file off the model numbers and other identifying marks, too, and sometimes paint the cars over. Now if somebody brought those cars we saw the other day with these tags on, from out West, and exchanged them here—see?"

"I see." Greg nodded eagerly. "I was right! I told you they were stolen cars the other day, when we first saw all those at the house on Boxwood, remember?"

"We didn't have all the data then that we have now." Ronny made some more notes, and then put away his notebook.

"Will we tell the police?"

"I guess we'll have to," Ronny said reluctantly, "though it would be great to solve The Case of the Stolen-Car Ring all by ourselves. But I'm afraid it comes under the head of what Dad would call dangerous. They might be desperate criminals, for all we know."

"Now can we find the frog?" Evie asked. Ronny could tell she didn't care a bit about the stolen-car ring—all she wanted was to open that trunk. Well, he was pretty curious himself about it.

"Come on, then." He led them inside the cluttered shed. "What do you see, my dear Watson? Miss Morstan? It is of the highest importance in the art of detection," he said solemnly in his Holmes voice, "to be able to recognize out of a number of things which are incidental and which vital."

"You wouldn't know either," Greg pointed out, "if you hadn't seen it in that paper."

"What do you see?" Ronny repeated. "It's right in front of your eyes, Evie. If it were any closer it could spit on you and make warts, that frog could."

"I don't see any frog."

"Actually there are three of them."

Before they could count anything in threes, to find out what it was he was talking so mysteriously about, they were startled by a voice behind them.

"Well, if it isn't Evie! Just the kid I want to see!"

They turned, drawing closer together instinctively. A man stood in the door, the kind of man Ronny's dad would have said to avoid. He was a tough-looking hombre, Ronny thought; he hadn't shaved and his shirt was dirty and he looked just plain mean. How could he know Evie?

Evie said hardily, "Well, I don't want to see you, Crane Lewis. We don't ever want to see you or your mean old brother Finch again."

"Your ma thought she had got away from Finch, didn't she? But she cashed his unemployment check —that's where she made her mistake. When Finch told the unemployment people it had been took and cashed without his permission, they naturally told him who cashed it. And she had to give her address when she cashed it, of course. So it wasn't hard to trace her."

"She didn't steal it! He gave it to her—before she decided to leave him. Before he hit her that last time —before she found out what he was doing—" Then she remembered. "Oh—so it's you and Finch," she said slowly, "in this stolen car ring—and those Jowers kids. But Finch couldn't have followed us here just for that—"

"He came after his kid," Crane Lewis said. "He wants his baby. That is," he added, "unless somebody wants to pay him to go away and let her keep the kid without him—"

"He knows my mother doesn't have any money."

"But," Crane Lewis said with a nasty sort of smile, "Finch somehow got the idea that your ma's dear mother who lives in Atlanta does have money. And the rocks your mother kept in that trunk of hers—they might do to pay Finch with, if she wants to keep the baby."

"Finch doesn't care anything about Joy. She wasn't even born—when we left—"

"How right you are. But the kid is a capital asset, if you know what I mean. She's negotiable. Finch can trade her for money—or the rocks. He wants her and he's going to get her. You're going to tell us where she is."

Ronny thought, I hope Mama didn't give Mrs. Garner or anybody around here our address. "No, we're not," he said, to give Evie what Dad called moral support. "And you'll never find her. And you're trespassing on this property. So you had better leave."

"Look who's talking," the man sneered. "Friend of yours, Evie?" He moved closer to the three of them. Ronny wished they had brought Froman, but Froman was off chasing cats. "Now you be a good kid, Evie, and give me the key to that house. We'd rather get in

with a key than risk 'breaking-and-entering.' Then we can get into the trunk and find what Finch wants— and he'll go away and let your mother keep the baby." He tried to speak enticingly, but Evie was hating him so much she couldn't even answer. She was fighting herself to keep from crying, but her big glassie-marble tears were spilling over.

"No!" Greg said, more bravely than he looked. "She's not about to give you anything. Don't you do it, Evie."

Ronny thought, his hand on a cracked flower pot on the shelf behind him, It's good we hadn't found the key to the trunk yet. He might take it by force—he's stronger than we are. He might take the house key from Evie, right now.

"Run, Evie!" he shouted, and threw the flower pot straight at the man's face. "Get outside! He won't try anything where people can see him! Run, Greg!" He himself was getting to the door, too—and fast, right behind Evie and Greg.

Crane Lewis was recovering from the sudden flower pot in his face. "Why, you little runt—" he yelled, "I'll make you sorry for that."

The three had gained the front of the lot, where what happened would not be screened from passers-by on the street. Crane Lewis followed them, but he was no longer threatening to touch them. Ronny knew he wouldn't do that as long as they were in the open.

"No, you won't," he said—and wondered in the back of his mind how come he was managing to keep his voice steady, when he felt so unsteady inside. Just as if he felt brave, when he didn't really. "You'll go away right now and leave Evie alone, and so will Finch, if you know what's good for you. Because we know all about the stolen cars, and we have the license numbers—in a safe place at home—that you exchanged on these cars here and those at the old house on Boxwood Avenue. And we're going to the police with them. Right away. So if you have any sense at all, you'll run!"

He hoped the threat would work. Logically, it ought to. But criminals weren't always logical. You'd have to be stupid or you wouldn't be a criminal. Crane Lewis might not believe him.

But the man did look startled—and maybe scared. Anyway, he muttered some kind of a cuss word Ronny had never heard before—but he was sure it was a cuss word—and ran to one of the cars and scratched off. To tell Finch, Ronny hoped, and try to make their getaway without bothering Evie any more.

"Whee!" Greg said. "He believed you. And the tag numbers aren't really in a safe place at home. They're right there in your pocket."

"That's all right—it was the right time and the right place, as Dad says, for a white lie. That crook believed it, and it saved us. He might have made Evie give him the key to the house, and then he'd have broken into the trunk and got the rocks—"

"What did he mean, rocks in the trunk?"

"Don't you know?" Ronny was smug with his own knowledge.

"Could we please," Evie said, getting her voice back at last, "find the key under the frog and see what's in the trunk, before he brings old Finch back here with him to get the other two cars? And the trunk? And—Joy?"

# The Key
# Under the Frog

Joy's safe," Ronny assured her. "Mama and Mattie won't let anybody get her. Froman won't either. Besides, that old Mr. Lewis doesn't know where she is."

"But some court or judge might say Finch has a legal right to her because he's her father. If I can't find my grandmother to fight for her as a natural guardian or something."

"If we get him put in jail for car stealing I don't think they'd give her to him," Ronny said. "He couldn't keep her in jail. What I do think is that he'll be scared to try anything else, because we know about the car stealing."

"But he might come back for the other cars. And to break open the trunk. So let's get the key."

They rushed back to the shed.

"Don't you see the three frogs?" Ronny said, but now he couldn't tantalize them any more, because there really was a need to hurry. "There they are."

"This is the only thing there are three of," Greg said doubtfully. He picked up a heavy, dusty piece of metal about two inches square, with prongs sticking up. There was nothing under it.

"Ladies call that thing a frog," Ronny said. "I saw a picture on the Women's Page, of a lady making a flower arrangement for a flower show, and it said she was putting the rose stems into the frog. It's a flower holder, see, to put in the bottom of the bowl to hold the stems and make them stand up. I wonder why they call it a frog, though."

"Funny thing to call it," Greg said.

Holding her breath, Evie reached for the other two lead frogs—one round and one oblong. The oblong one was upside down. Under it was something forced up into the prongs so that the frog stood flat and the object beneath was unnoticeable. It was a key.

"Whee!" Greg said. "You were right, Ron."

"Elementary, my dear Watson."

"So what did he mean by 'rocks in the trunk'?" Greg panted as they raced for the bedroom, Evie clutching the key.

"Rocks are what crooks call diamonds. Jewels. Evie, did your mother have jewels?"

"I don't know. I never saw any. But she had something he wanted. Could've been jewels for all I know."

Her hand shook as she tried to fit the key into the lock of the old trunk.

"Hurry!" Greg said.

"Hush, Greg. You'll make her nervous," Ronny said. "Want me to try, Evie?"

"No, thanks, Ron. I guess I ought to do it myself. Because maybe she would want me to."

At last she had the key in the hole. It was hard to turn—it seemed like forever to Ronny before she managed it. Then she lifted the lid.

It was an old-fashioned trunk, lined with faded paper resembling wallpaper, in a small pattern of tiny flowers and birds and animals. A shallow tray fitted across the top, like a shelf, concealing what lay below. A musty smell of age and closed-in-ness invaded their noses.

"It's nothing but a mess of papers," Greg said, disappointed.

"It must be her novel," Evie said soberly. "She once told be she was writing a novel, but she never let me read any of it. She worked on it late at night after I was in bed. She said it was the story of her life."

"Well, she must want you to read it now," Ronny said.

"Not now," Evie said. "Put it all in a sack and I'll take it to your house to read. We've got to hurry and get out of here, before Crane comes back with Finch."

"There must be something else underneath," Greg suggested. "How about taking out that tray thing?"

Ronny lifted it out. They stared into the trunk, at a curious and touching assortment of things a child-bride had taken when she ran away from home—far away—to get married.

Evie, after a moment of silence, said, "There's a broken piece of stained glass. If we ever find the gingerbread house, we can tell if it fits into any of the panes. She loved that house—she had to take a little piece of it with her. And there's a key that looks like an old house key! I bet it's the key to the gingerbread house!"

Ronny said solemnly, "Do you know what that big folded American flag means? It means your Uncle Sandy is dead. That's the way they fold the flag from a soldier's coffin to give it to his family. I saw our Great-uncle Aubrey's. That's why she cried when she thought about him."

"There's her cheerleader baton," Greg said. "But what the heck is this?" He leaned over and picked up

a slim, squared post that seemed made of white concrete, broken off at the bottom. Something had been crayoned on it.

Evie took it and read it, and her big round tears spilled down her cheeks. "It's Mittens's tombstone," she said, choking. "She told me she put a tombstone over his grave. Look what she wrote. 'Mittens. Born 1946. Died June 1, 1948. He was muched loved.' She was only ten then and couldn't spell very well. It's so sad I can't stand it!"

"Don't cry, Evie," Ronny said. "I guess when somebody you love dies you have to try to be glad you had him awhile, anyway. I would if it were Froman. It would have been worse if she hadn't ever had any pet at all to love."

"I s'pose you're right." Evie wiped her face on her arm, not having a handkerchief.

"Look what's on the back of it!" Greg said. "It must have been a street marker, that got broken off—and she used it for the tombstone!"

" 'North Avenue,' " Ronny read. "Now there's a real clue! The house has got to be somewhere near North Avenue, if not right on it. This narrows the search considerably, my dear Watson."

Greg was still looking in the trunk for more clues.

"Here's a little box." He handed it to Evie. She opened it. "What is it?"

"I don't know." She took the copper-colored medal out of the box. It was in the shape of a Maltese cross, dangling from a bar that had a screw-type thing like a tie-tac. "Looks like it was meant to wear on a coat lapel. It's a medal." She went on examining it. "Oh, it's another Confederate thing, see. On this side it says, 'Southern Cross of Honor.' And that wreath must be a laurel wreath. And '1861–65,' and a flag, and some words in a foreign language. '*Deo Vindice*'—if that's the way to pronounce it. I think it must be Latin—but I haven't had Latin yet."

"What's on the other side?"

"Another laurel wreath, and 'United Daughters of the Confederacy to the U. C. V.' and another Confederate flag."

"I bet U. C. V. means United Confederate Veterans," Ronny guessed. "Because the V in VFW means Veterans."

"So she had a Confederate veteran for a grandpa?" Greg said, wondering.

"More likely a great-grandpa. That war was a long time ago. And the Daughters of the Confederacy must have pinned each veteran with a 'cross of honor'—to let them know they appreciated what they did, even if they did lose the war." Ronny took the medal to examine it more closely. "First time I ever held one of these. I think most old soldiers wore their medals when they got buried." He turned it over. "Hey! Look. On the back of the bar there's a name engraved."

Evie took it and read, " 'Major Alexander Joyce. Atlanta. Patented.' "

" 'Patented' isn't part of the inscription, Evie," Ronny said. "It's doesn't mean Major Alexander Joyce was patented. It just means nobody else can make a Southern Cross of Honor but the U. D. C."

"But look!" Evie said excitedly. "It's a name! A whole name. The Alexander part must be where Uncle Sandy's name came from—your dad said Alexander was one it was a nickname for. And—Joy's name is Joyce. She was named for him too—whoever he was."

Ronny calculated rapidly. "He might have been your grandmother's grandfather. So she named her son—your Uncle Sandy—for him. Lots of people like to keep family names in the family."

"Then my mother," Evie said slowly, "might have been named for her grandmother? Christina Elizabeth?"

"Or that might even have been her mother's own name," Greg guessed. "Your grandmother's."

"I don't think so. It's too close. My mother was so awful careful not to leave anything around that would ever let anybody find out who she was. She'd've changed her name. Anyhow, if it were, it still wouldn't give us my grandmother's married name so we can find her now."

"Hey, we were about to miss this." Ronny reached into the corner of the trunk and carefully brought out a man's clean, folded handkerchief—yellowed; not new; worn from use and laundering.

"It's got embroidered initials," Evie said. "It must have been Uncle Sandy's, that she kept to remember him by. Look—I can almost read the initials. It looks like she embroidered it for him when she was just a little girl—it's not very good embroidery. I can do better than that—so she must have been younger than I am now, when she did it."

"What are the initials?" Ronny was impatient to see.

"Looks like A. J.—that would be for Alexander Joyce, I bet—and an F maybe? But it's frayed right there—it could have been some other letter. Well, it's better than nothing, I guess."

"Maybe when we read—when you read—" he corrected himself, "her novel, you will know a little more."

"Silly, you don't use real names in a novel. Then it would be a biography."

The trunk was empty now.

"There weren't any jewels after all," Ronny said, disappointed.

They were so absorbed in discovery that they didn't hear a car drive into the yard. Fortunately Greg glanced up and happened to look out the window.

"He's come back!" he whispered, as if the man could hear him even at a distance. "Evie—here's the sack —run—"

They had been putting the items, all but the tomb-stone which was too heavy, into the paper sack with the manuscript. Greg had the tombstone under his arm.

"Go out the front door and maybe he won't see you," Ronny said. "Hurry. We'll use delaying tactics and hang him up here while you get away with the stuff. If he sees you, go into Aunt Riah's—he won't dare follow you there. If we can lure him outside the front door here, you can get out of Aunt Riah's back door and go home without him following you."

"All right," Evie said. "Lock the house when you leave, Ron, will you? 'Bye now." She hurried, but Finch Lewis—it was a different ugly man, Ronny saw, so it must be Finch—caught a glimpse of her.

"Hey, Evie, you wait!" he shouted, but she made it to Aunt Riah's.

Ronny went to the back door and said politely, "Mr. Lewis? Is there anything we can do for you? Did you want to speak to Evie about something? She had to leave, but we're closing up the house for her."

It worked. The man pushed his way past Ronny and Greg, eager to get into the house, which gave Evie time to escape. Ronny knew she would be well on her way back to the Jamesons' by the time Finch Lewis had got over the empty trunk.

"Why, that little—!" he bellowed when he saw that she had taken everything from the trunk. "She got away with them! Where is she going, anyway? Where is she living?"

"Would you really like to know?" Ronny said daringly, just to keep him talking with the hope of finding out, giving Evie more time. He hoped Finch would keep on thinking Evie had the rocks—then he wouldn't search any more.

The man grabbed Ronny's shoulders and shook him. "You tell me where Evie is going with that stuff," he said menacingly, "or—"

"Take your hands off me," Ronny said. He was so mad he forgot to be afraid. "Or my father and the whole United States Army will sock it to you. Besides

the police. They've got the list of tag numbers of the cars you stole and exchanged tags on here and at the house on Boxwood Avenue. They'll be coming after you right away. Greg, maybe you'd better go next door and phone them to hurry it up—he might not be hanging around here too much longer."

"Right, Ron," Greg said. He knew Ronny meant for him to go home, since there was no phone at Aunt Riah's. He was near enough to the door to slip out before the man could grab him, though he made a lunge.

Finch Lewis turned back to Ronny. "Look, kid," he said, trying to be ingratiating, "I just want to get my family back together, that's all. The lady next door told me my wife is in the hospital, but she didn't know the address where Evie and the baby are staying. Now if you know—how would you like to make ten dollars?"

"Gee, Mister," Ronny said, trying to sound as if he were falling for the bribe, "ten dollars! Well—" The longer he could keep Finch talking, the better for Evie. He dragged it out.

"Here it is—take it," Finch Lewis urged. "Hurry up, kid—make up your mind. I got to get out of here." He glanced out the window, and Ronny did too. The other man and Bim Jowers were just getting into two of the cars, to drive them away.

Ronny took the ten dollar bill he held out—it was the only way to fool him—and said reluctantly, "Well, I promised Evie not to tell. But it's not exactly telling, is it, if I just say why don't you look for them at the Methodist Children's Home?" And that's no lie, he thought gleefully, when the man believed him. With a final angry look at the empty trunk, Finch Lewis hurried outside to get in the last of the cars and make his getaway. Ronny hoped he would detour by the Methodist Children's Home, which had just popped into his mind from nowhere. He thought it was way out in Decatur. Finch would probably tell them he was looking for his little girl who had run away and taken his baby with her. If he had any sense he'd know Evie wouldn't be over here in this part of town now, if she were living at the Home. But he didn't have much sense or he wouldn't be a criminal.

Well, he wouldn't find Evie and Joy. Ronny looked at the ten dollar bill in his hand, distastefully. He thought of tearing it up, but then decided it would be better to give it to Evie to buy some flowers to take to her mother in the hospital. A sick lady's no-good husband really ought to buy her some flowers, oughtn't he?

He shook the door after he closed it, to be sure it was locked, and ran all the way home. Evie and Greg, of course, had got there before him. Triumphantly, he gave them a dramatic version of how he had fooled Finch Lewis. "And he thinks you already found the rocks," he told Evie.

"Wish I had," Evie said. "I wonder what happened to them? Anyway, that was good thinking, Ron. And of course it'll be great to buy Mother flowers with the money. Good joke on Finch. Your mother called the hospital awhile ago, though, and she's no better. She might not even notice the flowers."

"Why don't you wait a day or two—maybe she'll be conscious again by then?" Mama suggested.

"I believe I will, Mrs. Jameson."

"Hey, Mama," Ronny said, "what should we do about the stolen car ring? Had I better give the tag numbers to the police right away?"

"I suppose you ought to," Mama said. "But I'd really rather you'd wait till tonight and consult your dad. He'll know exactly what's the best thing to do. I worry a little about your getting involved in informing on a bunch of criminals. They might try to get back at you somehow. Let's ask your dad."

"Okay," Ronny agreed.

"I kind of wish," Evie said, "that Finch could get away—and go somewhere a long way off, so Mother would never see him again."

"Why?" Greg said.

"Well—because after all, he's Joy's father, and it would be pretty awful to grow up with your father in jail. It'd be better not to have any father at all. And— he wanted Joy. Of course, he probably just wanted to use her like to sell to my grandmother, to get money— but what if he really wanted his baby? He can't have her, of course, but what if he loved her—a little bit, anyhow? I feel kind of sorry for him. But I'll never understand why my mother married him."

"Maybe you will—when you read her book," Ronny said. "But let's don't stop to read it till tonight. Right after lunch we're going to the Rhodes Memorial Hall and try to find out what your mother's name was when she won the history medal, remember?"

"I happen to have a free afternoon, for a change," Mama said, "and I'll drive you out to Rhodes Center. But we'll have to hurry home in time for Mattie to get off."

"Thanks, Mama! What's for lunch?"

"Hamburgers," Greg said. "I want three, Mama. Hey, Ron, did you forget about the street sign? I brought it home, you know." He gestured to the corner of the kitchen, where Mittens's tombstone was leaning.

"No, I didn't forget. But we can't do everything at once. You know my methods, Watson."

"Will we get out to North Avenue tomorrow, and look for the gingerbread house that fits the broken piece of stained glass?"

"I hope so," Ronny said. "If something more important doesn't come up. But of course, if we find out her name this afternoon, maybe we can get Evie's grandmother on the telephone."

"That would be wonderful," Evie said.

"That old phone book never did us any good yet," Greg grumbled.

When they climbed the high cement steps to the Rhodes Memorial with its gray stone walls and towers, Ronny said, "Wow! This is a neat building!"

"I don't know that I'd call it neat exactly." Mama laughed at his adjective. "It was one of Atlanta's finest old homes. I was told it was copied from a Bavarian castle."

"Old Mr. Rhodes must have really liked castles."

"I expect he did," Mama said. The massive door was open, and the hall inside looked dim and hushed, sort of like a church.

A lady at a desk near the door was looking at them questioningly. Mama recognized her as the Mrs. Baker she had met, and Mrs. Baker said she was glad to see her again. After Mama introduced the children, she let them do the talking.

"Can I do something for you?" Mrs. Baker asked encouragingly.

"Yes'm," Ronny and Evie said together, and Ronny went on, "Please. Evie, show Mrs. Baker your medal. We're trying to find out who won this medal in a contest, a long time ago, and a story in the paper said the U. D. C. had a kind of headquarters here to keep its records in; so we thought maybe you'd look it up and tell us the name of the girl that wrote the winning essay. It was before 1954—when she was in high school. You see, she was Evie's mother, but—"

Mrs. Baker looked at the medal, and then at Evie.

"I know it sounds crazy," Evie said, "but I need to know what my mother's name was before she married. She wouldn't ever tell me, and now she's in the hospital unconscious, and I need to find my grandmother, and I don't know her name, even—"

Mrs. Baker nodded as if she understood, Ronny thought, though it wasn't very clear. Old Evie got too excited trying to tell about it. He didn't believe he could explain it himself any better, though. It did sound weird.

"It's the Jefferson Davis medal," Mrs. Baker said. "It's been the prize in an historical essay contest in the high schools for many years."

"Yes'm. But have you got a record of who won it?"

"Some of the U. D. C. records are kept here," Mrs. Baker said, "but that would be in the minute books, and the president of the Georgia Division of the U. D. C.—Mrs. Alva Gordon—has all the minute books since 1934. So they'd be out at her house."

Evie looked as though she were about to cry with

disappointment. Ronny said hurriedly, "Could you tell us where Mrs. Gordon lives, please, Mrs. Baker?"

"I could, of course. But—child, I'm sorry—" to Evie, "the Gordons aren't at home right now. They're in Europe."

The big tears spilled over. "I can't help it," Evie sobbed. "Every time it looks as if we're about to find out, it turns out wrong. We'll never find my grand-mother!"

"Of course we will," Greg said. "Don't cry, Evie. We've still got North Avenue to look at."

"Why don't you children enter the essay contest yourselves this fall?" Mrs. Baker said. "It's a good sub-ject, about whether there should be only one Memorial Day instead of two—national Memorial Day on May 30 and Confederate Memorial Day on April 26—and whether the U. D. C. should decorate all the graves at the National Cemetery at Marietta—the Yankees too—as well as the ones in the Confederate Cemetery, on that one Memorial Day. It's in the interests of national unity, to combine and have only the one," she explained. "I think we should, myself. But you can write the essay from either point of view, of course. Evie, it would be nice, child, if you could win the Jefferson Davis medal too, since your mother did."

"Thanks, Mrs. Baker," Ronny said. "But we aren't

in high school yet. Maybe some other year, later, Evie might try it."

"Thanks, Mrs. Baker," Evie echoed dolefully.

Greg said, "Are you really a Daughter of the Confederacy, Mrs. Baker? You don't look exactly old enough."

Mrs. Baker laughed. "Yes, I belong to the organization, child. Nowadays it's not restricted to the daughters of Confederate veterans. We're all descended from veterans, though."

Mama said, "We'd better get back, so Mattie can get off on time. Come on, children."

"Good-by, Mrs. Baker," they said. "And thanks."

"I wish I could have helped," Mrs. Baker said.

As they got in the car, Greg asked, "Could we drive by North Avenue, Mama?"

"I'm afraid not today," Mama said, starting the car. "Sorry, but it's a long way out of the way. We've got to get on the South Expressway and go on home. So that'll have to wait."

Some little nudge of past knowledge had been trying to break through Ronny's consciousness, and at last he knew what it was.

"Hey!" he said excitedly, as they turned onto the Expressway, headed for home, "Evie, even if we didn't find out your mother's name, I think I know how we can find out your Uncle Sandy's!"

# The Clues
# in the Manuscript

Well, how?" Evie looked hopeful again, and Greg
urged Ronny with his elbow. "How? How?"

"You know my methods, Watson. This will require a
trip to the Post tomorrow on the bus. Or maybe if we
get up and get ready early Dad'll let us ride out there
with him."

"Why do we want to go to Fort Mac?"

"Because I think we need to consult the Chaplain.
You know, Dad told us that soldiers and their families
could always consult the Chaplain of any Army post
if they needed advice. And we need his advice."

"Sometimes I wish we'd never heard of Sherlock
Holmes," Greg muttered. "It makes you act so awful
mysterious, Ron."

"I'll tell you tomorrow." That was all he would say.

After supper Greg wanted Evie to read the manuscript from the trunk aloud to them, but Ronny saw how Evie looked—as if she didn't much want to—and told his brother, "No, Greg. I think Evie ought to read that first by herself, and then tell us what it says—if she wants to. It might be kinda private stuff."

"Okay," Greg said. Mama nodded.

"Right, Ron," Evie said, and her shoulders huddled up a little, as if she were scared of what the private stuff might be. She took the papers and went into the bedroom where Joy was sleeping, closing the door softly. The shaded lamp wouldn't wake the baby, and Ronny sensed Evie's feeling that she and Joy ought to be alone with this record of what her unconscious mother was trying to tell her.

Ronny and Greg told Dad about the stolen-car ring, and gave him the tag numbers. He called the police right away, and explained as well as he could, with the boys interrupting all the time to add more details. The sergeant on duty said he appreciated the boys' interest in upholding the law, and that it was right smart of Ronny to get the tag numbers. He'd put out a lookout notice immediately, and if the men were caught, he'd be in touch, for the boys and Evie to identify them.

That contact with the police was more exciting than watching TV—it was only reruns. They could hardly settle down to an old Bonanza episode after the promise of a real police lookout for stolen cars they had spotted.

After a while Evie came out, and Ronny could tell she had been crying. Greg turned off the television and looked at her expectantly. Ronny said hastily, "You don't have to tell us anything she wrote if you don't want to, Evie."

Though she looked troubled and unhappy, Evie braced her shoulders and said slowly, "I guess I've got to face it. Well, my father wasn't any hero—Mother made that story up just for me, about him getting drowned saving the kid. That is, if he was the guy in the novel—and she did say it was the story of her life. See, in the novel this girl's mother wanted her to wait and finish high school and go to college, and the girl loved a boy and didn't want to wait. Her mother told her the boy was no good, but she ran away and married him anyhow. And it turned out her mother was right. He got in trouble and got killed by a policeman. Right after the baby—that was me, I guess—was born. He was just a bum. But she was too proud to go back and let her mother know she was right about the boy. So she stayed on in California and worked. And after a while she married another guy—and when he turned out the same way, another bum, why, she thought there must be something wrong with her or she wouldn't like the wrong kind of men. She went to a psychiatrist, and he told her she had a guilt complex on account of not obeying her mother—that she was unconsciously punishing herself by marrying bad guys. And he told her the thing to do was leave the bad guy and go back to her mother and admit she was wrong and had made a mistake, and start over. But the girl was still too stubborn and proud to tell her mother she'd found out that her mother was right. She got as far as coming back to the same town, but she wanted to be a success—a great writer or rich or something—before she let her mother know she was here. And she couldn't. The book isn't finished—I guess she still hoped she could find a happy ending. But you see, it tells why she wouldn't let even me know who she was. She knew I'd probably get in touch with my grandmother as soon as I was old enough to dial a phone or write a letter. So she never put any name in for the girl's mother, in case I ever accidentally saw the novel. And no last name for the girl or her brother. Just Christina and Sandy."

"It just shows," Greg said, "you ought to admit it when you make a mistake."

"But I can see how hard it would've been, for a proud person like my mother," Evie said slowly. "And how awful it was for her, because she loved her mother and her home and all so much. You could tell by the way she wrote in the novel that she wished she could go back and have everything like it used to be. She was always fighting it out with herself—and her mother never won. But she might have, if— See, she did come back here. So that means she might have— after a while—decided to see her mother again. If she hadn't got hit by that car. She was thinking about it, I know. She couldn't know she'd get in the hospital. And—it means I've just got to find my grandmother, and tell her how Christina loved her and wanted to come back."

"We'll find her," Ronny promised. "We've got to. See, Christina couldn't tell her because it was all her fault and she was too proud to admit it—but she'd really be awfully glad if somebody else did and she couldn't help it. She'd be mighty happy after it was done, if you did it."

"The only reason the girl in the novel wasn't sorry she married those bad guys," Evie said, her voice shaking a little, "was because she had the kids. Us. Joy and me. She never was sorry she had us, and she wouldn't give us up for adoption or put us in foster homes or anything, no matter how hard she had to work to make a living for us. So I've got to do that for her— find my grandmother. Not just to take care of Joy and me—but to get her mother and Christina back together. It's funny—sometimes I think of Christina like another girl, not my mother at all. And I want—so much—for her story to have a happy ending."

Mama had been listening, and she said gently now, "Evie—darling—we're all going to help you until you find your grandmother. And I'm sure your mother will be glad."

"Thanks, Mrs. Jameson. You're all being real good."

Ronny said, "Dad, can we go to the Fort with you tomorrow? We've got another lead—a clue to Uncle Sandy's last name, that we want the Chaplain to help us with. Who's the Chaplain now anyway? Is Major Duncan still there? I remember that Sunday you took us to the Chapel and we met him."

"No. He was transferred. There's a Major Trent now. Yes, I'll take you. But—what are you going to ask him about?"

"Aw, Dad, I don't want to tell you about it. I want to see if it's a good clue, first. But if I'm right, we'll know Uncle Sandy's last name pretty soon. We already know he was Alexander Joyce something. You saw the medal and the handkerchief."

"Oh, I forgot," Evie said. "There was something else besides the novel. I know my great-grandmother's first names. She was Christina Elizabeth, too. My mother was named for her mother's mother, you see."

"How'd you know?"

"It wasn't part of the novel, but in with the papers there was a half-finished letter my mother was writing to her mother a long time ago—but she never mailed it. It was dated in 1960. It told about the jewels."

"Wow!" Ronny said, getting excited. "What about them? Hurry—I can't wait!"

"They've gotta be somewhere," Evie said, "because she never sold them. We never had any money. And they're very valuable. And Finch was still expecting to find them in the trunk.

"See, my mother's grandmother she was named for left her family jewels to be given to Christina Elizabeth when she was twenty-one—a diamond-and-ruby necklace and some other things, but the necklace sounded like it was what my mother thought was the most valuable. But Christina ran off before she was twenty-one. She didn't really have any right to take the jewels, though they would belong to her some day —and that was another thing she felt guilty about, I guess—but she did. She got them out of her mother's drawer and took them with her. She was writing her mother about being sorry she did that. I wonder why she never sent the letter. Still too proud, I guess, to admit she'd made another mistake. Anyhow, she didn't sell them, I'm pretty sure."

"So they're still at your house?" Dad mused. He frowned. "That's not very safe—to leave anything valuable in an unoccupied house, even if it is hidden. And it does sound as though those things might be quite valuable. Would you like for me to try to help you find them, Evie?"

"Yes, sir, please. But we looked everywhere already. Mother seemed to be trying to tell me to find the key and look in the trunk. But you know we took everything out of the trunk and there weren't any jewels. Finch seemed to think they were there, too. But they weren't."

"Finch thinks Evie got them," Ronny explained. "I fooled him about that so he would go away and not look any more."

"Well, it wouldn't hurt to look again around the house, I suppose."

"Now, Dad?" Greg said eagerly. "Right now?"

Mama said, "You all ought to be in bed."

"But this is so important," Ronny said earnestly.

"I think we ought to go tonight," Dad said to Mama, "even if it is late, because those men might decide to look again—or other people might come plundering and find them accidentally—and an unoccupied house isn't a safe place for anything to be left in, especially in that neighborhood. So—come on, men. Evie."

They piled into the station wagon, and Froman came too. They couldn't exactly hide him—he was too big—but Dad didn't say no. After Froman licked the back of his neck a couple of times, though, and nearly made him run into a telephone pole, he told Ronny he'd have to put Froman out if the dog couldn't sit back on the seat and act like a civilized person. After that Ronny and Greg got Froman between them and each put an arm around him, which anchored him fairly well.

When they got out at the house, Evie said, "I'd better go tell Aunt Riah it's only us—she might get upset if she saw the lights on."

"We'll wait for you," Ronny said.

She came back and reported. Aunt Riah said there hadn't been anybody bothering around at all since the cars were taken away that morning. "She says Finch and Crane are a long way from here by now. She put a bad luck spell on them, though; so they'll have a lot of trouble, she says. Like flat tires and stuff. And maybe they'll get snake-bit, because she used some ground-up rattlesnake rattles in the spell."

"I don't really think we should depend on that snake-bite bit," Ronny said, "but they might have a flat tire. Easy. The way they park in old back yards where there might be planks with rusty nails in them."

"And Aunt Riah says we'll find something valuable tonight," Evie said. "That must be the necklace. She had a dream that we did. She says that kind of dream of hers—between moondown and sunup—never fails. But I guess we shouldn't depend on that too much, either."

She opened the door with her key, and showed the boys' father where the trunk was.

"It's still empty," Greg pointed out.

"Well, let's look everywhere else where there might have been a hiding place," Dad said. "Evie's mother could have decided to put the jewelry somewhere else, and then when she was only half conscious she might have remembered only where it was hidden originally."

They searched everywhere. Dad even poked around the floorboards, as if he thought she might have fixed a hiding place underneath, but there were no signs that the ancient floor had ever been disturbed. He even looked for loose bricks in the mantel-facing and the hearth, but everything was solid. He tapped the walls as if they might be hollow and have a space like

a secret closet behind them. But there was nothing like that. He explored drawers and the backs of the pieces of furniture, explaining that she could have taped a box out of sight there. But there was no box. Nothing.

The children helped look, but though Ronny admitted they hadn't thought of all those places Dad did, they gave up before he did.

"It's no use, Dad," Ronny said gloomily. "Evie's mother was just smarter at hiding things than we are about finding them."

Dad was staring down into the empty trunk, and they all gathered around and stared too.

"One time," Ronny said, "I read about a man named Dr. Peters who could materialize things—make them appear—just by thinking about them. It proved the control of mind over matter, whatever that means. If we had him here, maybe he could materialize Christina Elizabeth's diamond-and-ruby necklace."

Dad said, "Tell me again, Evie, just what it was your mother said when you saw her in the hospital. About the key and the trunk."

"All I could make out," Evie said, "was that she was muttering about 'key—trunk—look under the frog.' That was all."

"Those exact words? And that was all?"

"Yes, sir. 'Key—trunk—look under the frog.' So we did finally find the frog in the shed, and looked under it, and there was the key, like she said. So—she must have meant for us to look for the other things we found in the trunk. Not the diamonds and rubies. Because they weren't here."

"Hey!" Greg said suddenly. He was so excited he could hardly speak. "I see something! I bet—it could be—"

"What?" Ronny demanded.

"My dear Holmes," Greg said tantalizingly, getting his voice back, "I believe I'll wait till tomorrow to tell you."

# The Rocks
# in the Trunk

Greg couldn't hold out, of course—he was so eager to see if he really had guessed where the jewels were that he had to tell them right then.

"See, Dad," he began, "and Evie and Ronny, if you look real close at this wallpaper the trunk is lined with, it has all kinds of stuff on it—flowers and bees and squirrels and bugs and deer and—AND—over in that corner there's a frog! Now what if Evie's mother had meant two frogs—to look under two different frogs? After we found the key under one—look under the other for the diamonds?"

"Greg, I believe you've got it!" Dad said. He was already stripping the pasted-down piece of paper with the frog on it from the inside of the trunk. "Yes—

look! I should have thought of a false bottom!" Under the frog on the pattern there was a light depression in the thin strip of wood that seemed to be the bottom of the trunk. The slit made a place where fingers could pull. With the boys and Froman leaning over him and Evie on her knees beside the trunk, holding her breath and clutching the edge with her hands, Dad tucked two fingernails into the slit and drew the thin wood back. Half of it slid under the other half. There was a compartment underneath. In it was a pale-blue velvet box. The velvet was so old it had faded almost to gray.

Evie gasped, "It's—it's a jewelry box. It's the first Christina Elizabeth's—that she wanted my mother to have!"

Dad lifted it out and handed it to her. There was a small silence. Evie seemed reluctant to open the box. Greg said, "Hurry!" Dad told her gently, "And it would seem your mother wanted you to find it."

At last Evie opened the box.

"Wow!" Ronny shouted. "Look at the rocks!"

"It looks like a diamond-and-ruby dog collar for a big dog like Froman," Greg said wonderingly.

It was a beautiful old-fashioned necklace, the kind that fitted high around the throat—linked gold-backed squares, each centered by a ruby surrounded with diamonds, and one larger than the rest pendant in the

center. The stones glittered with magic fire although the gold was darkened.

"There are earrings, too," Evie said, lifting out the necklace. "And some rings. There's one with an emerald, I guess—it's green. And look at the diamond pin. Cool!"

"They called it a brooch," Dad said, examining it with interest. "These things are magnificent, Evie. We'd better put them in a safe-deposit box at the bank, tomorrow."

"I guess so, sir. Would you—please?"

"I will. First thing."

"Thanks, Captain Jameson."

Ronny said, "Well, if you're going to report to your office before you do it, Dad, we can still go with you, can't we? Because even if we did find the rocks, we still have to find out Uncle Sandy's last name, so we can find Evie's grandmother."

"All right. I suppose I should see about a few things at the office first."

Greg was still admiring the necklace, trying to put it around Froman's neck, until Evie snatched it away from him. "It's *not* a dog collar," she said severely.

Ronny said, "No wonder old Finch wanted this stuff. She shouldn't have let him know about it—it must have just slipped out when she didn't mean to tell him.

I bet he could sell it for at least a million dollars."

"Not that much," Dad said. "But it's surely worth a thousand or two."

"And my mother didn't sell it," Evie said proudly. "Even when we needed money so bad, she kept the things her grandmother wanted her to have. Even after she got to be twenty-one and they were really hers."

"Your mother's all right," Ronny said.

Evie put the jewelry back in the box and handed it to Dad to keep for her.

"We'd better get home with this treasure trove," he said. "There was a holdup at a parking lot not far from here last week."

As Evie locked the door, she said, "Do we have time, sir, for me to run over and tell Aunt Riah she dreamed right? That we did find it? And show it to her?"

He gave her back the box. "Sure. She deserves that much, for dreaming us luck."

Evie came back and said Aunt Riah promised to dream as hard as she could, next time, that they would find her grandmother. "And she said the rocks were gorgeous. She said sometimes a toad's head has a ruby in it, but she never found one like that. It's good luck if you do."

"Ha. I reckon it is," Greg said.

"Wait a minute!" Ronny said, as Dad was putting the velvet box back into his inside pocket. "Will you, Dad? I want to ask her to dream something for me." Dad sighed, but waved him on. Ronny came back and reported, "She's going to try to dream tonight that we find out Uncle Sandy's name tomorrow."

"I wish she'd just dream what it is," Greg said. "She could save us a lot of trouble."

When Dad dropped them next morning at the Chaplain's office in the old Post Headquarters building, he said, "Here's bus fare back home. And you'll keep in touch, won't you? Report in at lunchtime, so your mother won't worry about you?"

"Sure, Dad. Thanks. But we might get hung up. If we do, we'll call her, though." Ronny wasn't feeling nearly as confident as he tried to appear about his new idea and its chance of producing results. He knew it was a good idea, but he was uncertain how they were going to work it out exactly. That's what he hoped the Chaplain would help him with.

" 'Bye, Dad," Greg said, and Evie added, "Thanks for bringing us, sir."

"Well, Ron, are you going to tell us now?" Greg demanded as Dad drove away. "Before we go in to see the Chaplain? It's not fair."

"Yes, please tell us, Ron," Evie said.

"Well, okay. It was the folded flag, see, and Mrs. Baker mentioning the National Cemetery at Marietta, that made me think of it. If your Uncle Sandy was killed in Korea, and they brought his body home, and buried him with military honors like they do when they have a flag on the coffin, well, more than likely he was buried in that National Cemetery. Dad has a picture of an American military cemetery at Saint-Avold—that's in France—where our Great-uncle Aubrey, who was killed in the Battle of the Bulge, is buried, and it has crosses with the names of the soldiers on them. So—if they do that same way at Marietta—and if his first two names were Alexander Joyce and the last initial was something like an F, like on the handkerchief, why, we could look and maybe—"

"I see!" Evie said. "Maybe there wouldn't be a whole lot of names beginning with Alexander J. It's not as if his name were John."

"You mean," Greg said, getting tired already, "that we have to look at all the tombstones till we find it?"

"Well, that's one way. It wouldn't be impossible, if we divided it up in three parts and each one looked at one section of the cemetery. But I wanted to ask the Chaplain if there's some other way—maybe a file at the cemetery showing who's buried where, you know—"

"It might even be alphabetical!" Evie was getting excited now. "So we wouldn't have to look too long—just in the Fs."

"We aren't sure that letter is an F," Ronny reminded her. "But anyway, let's ask the Chaplain how they do about the names of soldiers buried in the National Cemetery."

The door to the Chaplain's outer office was open. They hesitated until a corporal who was typing at the desk looked up. "Well, good morning," he said smiling. "What can we do for you?"

He was a good-natured-looking young corporal, with red hair and blue eyes and a few freckles. The sign on his desk read, *Chaplain's Assistant.*

"What does a chaplain's assistant do?" Greg was curious.

Ronny frowned at him. "You say good morning first," he told his brother. "Good morning, Corporal—" He looked at the name on the corporal's uniform shirt pocket, and couldn't help laughing. "Corporal Major?"

The young man laughed too. "That's right. Dan Major. It gives all the men a lot of laughs. And," he said to Greg, "what I do is everything except preach. I sweep out the office and the Chapel, and type the letters, and get the Chaplain's newspaper, and arrange the flowers when the ladies don't do it, and go to the post office and buy stamps, and even arrange details of funerals sometimes when the Chaplain's off duty. But he does the sermons."

"Well, maybe we won't have to bother Major Trent, then," Ronny said. "Maybe you know what we want to ask. You see, we—Greg and I—are Captain Jameson's sons. I'm Ronny. Dad's in Special Services here at the Post. Maybe you know him?"

"I may have run into him," Corporal Major mused, "though at the moment I can't exactly place the Captain. But any son of a captain is a friend of mine. So—"

"And this is Evie Hollis," Ronny said.

"Hi, Evie," the corporal said.

"Hi."

"Well," Ronny went on, "we have to find Evie's grandmother, and her mother's unconscious in the hospital and can't tell Evie her name. We called this morning before we left, and she's still unconscious. But Evie's Uncle Sandy, who'd've had the same last name, was a soldier who was killed, and we deduced it must have been in Korea sometime in about 1953 or like that, and we thought he might have been buried at the National Cemetery at Marietta. We know his first two names were Alexander Joyce, and we think his last initial might have been F. But we aren't sure. Now what we want to know is, how can we find out what a soldier named Alexander Joyce something's last name was if he was buried at the National Cemetery?"

"We were going to ask the Chaplain," Greg said.

"The Chaplain's off today. His mother's sick in Augusta and he went over there. But let me think. It might take some research. There were lots of men buried out there in 1953."

"Please, it's very important," Evie said, and her mouth had that desperate look again, and Ronny hoped she wouldn't cry those big tears. "If I don't find my grandmother, somebody might take Joy—that's my baby sister—away from me. If—if Mother doesn't get well, Joy's all I've got. Please—I need to find my grandmother so nobody can separate me and Joy."

Corporal Major gave her a sympathetic look. "It may be hard," he said, "to find the name, but it doesn't sound impossible. I've got an idea. Wait while I call Captain—Jameson, did you say? In Special Services?"

"Right," Ronny said.

They waited, wondering what he was going to say while he got through to Dad. "Captain, this is Corporal Major, in the Chaplain's office. Your sons and their friend are here, you know, sir, and they need some information from the National Cemetery at Marietta. It so happens that I have to drive out there this morning, since the Chaplain's away, to see about a funeral for tomorrow. Would you give permission, sir, for them to go along? I'll be driving a jeep from the motor pool."

He nodded and winked at the children as he listened to the Captain's answer. "Right. Thank you, sir." He hung up. "It's okay. We're to be careful, though." He grinned.

"In a real jeep?" Evie sounded thrilled.

"Aw, that's nothing," Greg told her. "We've ridden in jeeps lots of times."

"Well, I haven't," Evie said.

"You'll love it," Corporal Major said dryly.

Ronny knew what he meant. "It's not really very rough riding, Evie," he said. "I kinda like it myself. Anyhow, it'll be great to get out to Marietta and find out about your Uncle Sandy. And I bet"—he nodded confidently at the corporal—"the people in charge of things likes files and records, out there, will be a lot more likely to let a man in uniform from the Chaplain's office of the Third Army look at their stuff than just three kids."

"My thought exactly," the corporal told him. "Come

on, then. I already got the jeep from the motor pool. There wasn't a staff car left—at least, that's their story." He lifted Evie into the front seat beside the driver, while the boys scrambled into the back. "We'll take the four-lane to Marietta. Should make it in about an hour."

Evie wasn't doing much talking—she had her hands clenched again, Ronny noticed—so while they were on the way he told the corporal all about their search up until now.

"So when you find out Evie's uncle's name, then you're going to try to find her grandmother by telephoning everybody by that name in the phone book?" he said. "I hope it doesn't turn out to be Smith or Jones."

"The handkerchief clue looked like an F," Ronny reminded him. "But it was worn right there so we couldn't be sure."

"Well, let's see." The corporal was getting more and more interested in solving the puzzle, too. "If the edges of the letter were worn off, it could've been a B, or an R, or an E, or a P. Those are about the only letters with a bar in the middle like an F."

"That's right," Ronny said. "I didn't think of that. So if the list is by years and alphabetical, that cuts down where we have to look. Evie, we're getting warm! I have a feeling we're about to find out your grandmother's name."

"I hope," Greg said not too optimistically, "Aunt Riah dreamed right last night."

As they piled out of the jeep, Corporal Major lifting Evie and her crutch out, Ronny said, "Is a soldier in charge of the cemetery? Or maybe a retired soldier?"

"There's a lady named Mrs. Thompson in charge of the office," the corporal told him, "but I don't think she's a retired Wac. There's a superintendent too, but Mrs. Thompson's the one to see. She's okay; she won't give us any trouble."

He introduced the children to Mrs. Thompson, saying the boys were Captain Jameson's sons, but not bothering to say why they were along. Ronny surmised the corporal was just letting her think they came for the ride while he was coming on Chaplain's official business. The corporal knew his way around, all right. He had better sense than to try to tell her the whole story; that would've delayed things. He simply said in his brisk, matter-of-fact military manner, "I'd like to see your file of burials in 1953 and thereabouts, Mrs. Thompson. It might even be 1951 or 1952. But I'll look at 1953 first. I'm looking for a name—to see if a certain man killed in action in Korea was buried here."

As he had predicted, Mrs. Thompson gave him no trouble. She hunted up the 1953 card file, offered him a table in the outer office to work on, and went back to her desk in the next room.

Breathlessly the children hung over him while he flipped through the cards. "Might as well try F first," he said.

"There's an A." Ronny spotted it. "No—that's Allen—"

"There's not a single Alexander," Evie said.

"Don't give up yet, Evie. We've still got B and R and P and—what was that other letter? E. And the files of the other years of that war, too, if we don't find it in 1953."

Corporal Major said, "He could've been killed in one year and brought back in another. Here, Evie, you turn through them. I think you ought to be the one. And it won't seem so discouraging if you're doing something yourself to work out the problem. I'll go finish my business with Mrs. Thompson while you look."

"Okay. Thanks." She took his place in front of the file.

"Try B," Ronny urged.

"There's an Alexander." Greg pointed excitedly. "Oh, no—his middle initial is O."

"That middle one on the handkerchief couldn't have

been anything but a J," Evie said. "The monogram wasn't worn off till it got to the last letter. —Well, that's all the Bs."

"R, then?"

There was no Alexander in the Rs, and only one A—for Arnold. And only two—Abe and Andrew—in the Ps. Evie looked as if this were the last chance as she turned to the Es—though Ronny reminded her again about the other years it might have been.

"I just can't stand it if we get disappointed another time," Evie muttered, her head bowed over the file. Her fingers moved the cards slowly as she read the names one by one, shaking her head sadly over each.

"It's not here," she said at last. "That's the last one in E." One of her big tears rolled down and splashed on the table.

"No, it's not!" Ronny said. "You turned two at once, I think, Evie. I thought I saw—yes, you did!"

He poked the last card back. "And—this is it! Look —it's you, Evie! Like your mother said about the hairbrush monogram, remember, when she was teasing you? You thought she meant U instead of X or Z. But she meant you! It's you!"

# The Clue
# at the Cemetery

The name on the card was *Alexander J. Evelyn.*
There was some more stuff about things like when
and where he was killed in action—Ronny noticed it
was at Pyongyang and that he was a sergeant—but he
knew that all Evie saw was her uncle's last name.

"I get it!" Greg said. "Y-O-U, Evie. Your name. Evelyn."

Evie still looked stunned. Then she got her voice
back. "Of course! Mother gave us both family names.
Joyce—and Evelyn. So we could still belong to her
family—even if we didn't know we did."

"It was clever of your mother," Corporal Major said.
He had come back in time for the discovery. "She
didn't want you to lose identity with the family—and

the name was a clue, of course, if only you had been able to read it. She might have thought you'd guess, when you got older."

"I should have guessed, when we found the Confederate medal and saw that Joy was named a family name," Evie said.

"I bet that was what the C. E. on the painting was for," Ronny surmised. "She didn't mean Christina Elizabeth. She meant Christina Evelyn."

"Yes," Evie said. "And—of course! In the hospital! That was what she was trying to tell me, when she was saying Evelyn instead of Evie."

"Hey," Greg said, "now that we've found it, we'd better hurry home or we'll be late for lunch."

"I've got to get back to the office, too," Corporal Major said.

"Could we just hunt up *Evelyn* in the telephone book first?" Evie begged, looking around for it. "There couldn't be too many people with that last name." She saw the phone book on a desk and made a dive for it, dropping her crutch in her excitement. Ronny picked it up for her.

She couldn't turn the pages fast enough. Ronny and Greg hung over her as she hunted. Evans . . . there were two columns of Evanses. Evelyn. . . . There were four Evelyn's beauty shops and one Evelyn's dress shop and one Robert J. Evelyn and—Mrs. Alexandra Evelyn.

"There she is!" Evie was certain. "See—she's got a family first name, too, sort of. She was named for her father, I guess, or her grandfather, whichever Major Alexander Joyce was."

Ronny had his notebook out, taking down the address. "She lives at 2505 North Avenue Northeast," he said. "At last! We know exactly where the real gingerbread house is."

"We already knew that it was somewhere around North Avenue, from Mittens's tombstone, and there was 250 on the post in the picture," Evie said. "But it's great to have the whole address—and my grandmother's name and phone number."

Corporal Major was looking very unhappy, after he heard the address. "I do hate to tell you this, Evie," he said, "but I guess you ought to be prepared for maybe being disappointed again. That section of North Avenue, I'm pretty sure, is the section I saw pictures of in *The Atlanta Journal* the other day, where they're tearing down all the houses to build the freeway to Stone Mountain. The section of North Avenue between Moreland Avenue and Page Avenue, it said, in

Little Five Points. I thought what a shame it was those old houses had to go."

"Oh, no!" Ronny said. "Not after we've found it—"

"Did the pictures have a lot of gingerbread houses?" Greg asked.

"They were all old houses," the corporal said, "and some of them had gingerbread. But what I'm trying to tell you is, they were torn down. The pictures were showing how sad it was for the old homes to be 'gone with the wind' and hardly anything left but piles of— well, gingerbread and staircases and bricks and stuff."

Evie's big tears splashed on the phone book. "Do you s'pose," she asked, "Mrs. Thompson would let me use her phone? It wouldn't hurt to try this number— see, it's a 522 exchange, just like Mother used to dial and then hang up after my grandmother said 'Hello.'"

"Sure," the corporal said sympathetically. "But hurry, Evie. I've really got to report in soon, and I want to drop you kids off at home first." Ronny could tell he didn't expect she'd get any answer.

Mrs. Thompson gave her permission, of course. Evie dialed the number and waited; but Ronny knew it was no use when he saw the round tears roll down her cheeks again. She hung up slowly. "It's been disconnected," she said hopelessly.

"Well, we'll go there this afternoon, anyway," Ronny

said comfortingly. "Maybe some of the houses aren't torn down yet. They can't do them all at once, you know."

"But—my grandmother isn't there, if—"

"Well, somebody must know where she is. Now that we have her name and address we can find her."

"She probably left a forwarding address at the post office," Corporal Major said. "Ask at the Little Five Points' branch post office."

"I'm sure she's still alive," Evie said, not sounding at all sure, "because of Mother coming back here. I know she must have come to be close to her mother, even if she might have planned just to walk by the house some time and see her at a distance—or from the back of a church or something. And she wouldn't have come at all unless she knew my grandmother was still alive. She did that phone bit just before we left California, too."

"So let's hurry home and get lunch," Greg said, "so we can go to Little Five Points quicker."

They thanked Mrs. Thompson and left her wondering, Ronny thought, what it was all about. But she didn't ask, because after all Corporal Major was the Chaplain's assistant and he had come on official business.

The corporal thought the old road might be a short

cut back, instead of the four-lane with all the traffic, but he was wrong.

"We could hurry faster," Greg mumbled, "if big old stuff like that didn't get ahead of us." There was a wide load ahead that looked like a whole regular house on wheels.

"They ought not to be allowed to move houses in the daytime," Corporal Major said, agreeing. "They ought to wait till after midnight at least, when there's not much traffic. Here I am late for chow already. I'm going to turn off here and get on the four-lane after all."

"Don't you know the mess sergeant?" Greg said sympathetically. "He might fix you up a snack, if you miss chow."

"Aw, he can eat with us," Ronny said. "I think Mama was going to fix peanut-butter-and-jelly sandwiches today."

"Thanks, Ronny, but I'll get a bite at the PX snack bar. I've got to report in."

"They have good milk shakes, all right." Ronny didn't blame him.

The four-lane did get them home quicker. "Well, we sure do thank you for taking us to Marietta, Corporal Major. It was a big help," Ronny said as he and Greg hopped out of the jeep. The corporal lifted Evie down.

"Yes, I sure do thank you," Evie said. Her lips trembled, but she managed a smile.

"I hope you'll find your grandmother, Evie. I'm sure you will," Corporal Major said. As he drove off he called back, "I'll keep my fingers crossed."

"It'll be kinda hard for him to type with his fingers crossed," Greg said, and they all began to giggle, Evie a bit hysterically.

Joy was awake, and Evie changed her and held her while Ronny and Greg helped Mama fix the sandwiches and milk, and told her all about the morning's search and the address in Ronny's notebook, and about the phone being disconnected. "And can we go this afternoon and see if the gingerbread house is still at 2505 North Avenue Northeast?" Ronny said. "Can we, Mama?"

"I can't," Mama said. "I'm sorry, but I've got an appointment with the dentist, and you know how long we have to wait for those. If you can wait till I get back—but it might be too late. If you'll be careful, I guess you can go on the bus. There's a transfer downtown, but I think you're old enough now to ask somebody if you need help. The bus driver on the one you take from the shopping center will tell you exactly where to catch the one to Little Five Points."

"Right," Ronny said. "Sherlock Holmes and Dr.

Watson never had any trouble getting about London."

"But I don't believe it ever told exactly how they went," Greg said. "It just said they went."

"I think they used hansom cabs," Ronny said, "whatever those were."

"Good-looking cabs?"

"Not handsome, hansom, my dear Watson. H-a-n-s-o-m. The distinction is clear."

"Not very," Greg muttered.

Mama laughed. "Look it up, Dr. Watson. The dictionary is a useful tool—especially for Sherlock's assistant."

"I will later, Mama. I'm hungry right now."

Evie didn't eat much. Ronny knew how disappointed she was. Once she stopped and swallowed and asked Mama, "Did you happen to check with the hospital, Mrs. Jameson?"

"Yes, dear. They say her condition is fair, but there's no real change. I spoke to the floor nurse. Would you like to call yourself?"

"No'm. That's all right. Thanks." Evie took a swallow of milk, slowly, but left most of her sandwich.

Ronny finished his and said, "Any ice cream?" Evie liked ice cream, especially chocolate.

For once Mama didn't say "Eat it all." She must know how Evie felt. She gave them chocolate ice cream. Evie ate most of hers, Ronny was glad to see. He and Greg ate all theirs, of course.

"Well, let's go," Greg said.

Evie seemed reluctant, now that they knew where to go.

"What's the matter, Evie? Don't you want to go and at least look for the house?"

"I guess so. But—Ronny, I'm scared. I'm scared it won't be there."

"I know it is," Ronny said stoutly, though he didn't really feel sure at all. "Bring the piece of stained glass. In case we find a broken window that it fits. It's a clue. And the house number might be lost. Bring the house key we found in the trunk, too."

Evie went and got them, and held the stained-glass fragment in her hand while they walked to the bus stop. It's like a talisman, Ronny thought. If she holds onto that, maybe everything will come out all right. She had put the key in her pocketbook.

They transferred to the other bus without any trouble. The bus driver was very helpful, letting them off at the corner where the two-thousands began. They stood on the corner and stared around, not very hopefully. It looked like pictures of war ruins in Europe where cities had been bombed. The freeway was coming through, all right, and everything in its path had to go, Ronny knew. But like the corporal said, it was a shame. All these houses had been homes—where families lived and yellow roses grew and kids played and dads came home to supper and mothers called the kids in and puppies were born and cats died and were buried, with tombstones and forget-me-nots. . . . It was a shame to destroy homes.

"Look!" Greg said. "Those houses over there haven't got torn down yet."

"And there's one—" Evie said excitedly, "that looks just like that old house on Boxwood where the Jowers kids were—with the old cars. It looks like the picture in Mother's album! See the columns and the steps and all—hurry—"

"It's got oak and chinaberry trees and boxwood," Ronny said as they scooted down the sidewalk and across the yard of the old gingerbread house, and stopped suddenly in front of the steps. Somehow the house looked as if nobody was home. Or would ever be home again. Yet the windows still had curtains and draperies, and there were old rocking chairs on the porch.

"The number," Greg said solemnly, "is 2505. This is it."

"Numbers can be changed, remember?" Ronny cau-

tioned. "Don't be too sure. We've got to confirm all the details."

Evie straightened her shoulders in that way she had when she had to do something, and got herself up the steps on her crutch, determinedly. "There's the stained glass in the door," she whispered. "And it's in diamond shapes. And there's a rose vine at the end of the porch."

"But it's not blooming," Greg said, "so we can't tell if it's yellow."

"I know it's yellow," Evie said positively.

"There's no broken place in the stained glass," Ronny discovered.

"The broken place is probably in the window on the stair landing where she played dolls," Evie said. She hesitated a moment, then straightened her shoulders again and knocked at the door. It had an old-fashioned knocker of darkened brass, made like a boy's and a girl's faces—and when you knocked, the boy kissed the girl. "I wonder why she didn't tell me about the knocker," Evie said. "I bet she loved it, too."

Nobody answered the knock. She made the boy kiss the girl half a dozen times, but nobody came.

"I think we ought to open the door with that key that was in the trunk," Ronny said, "if it fits. We've gotta be sure—"

"Yes," Evie said. "I know we've got to. I'm just scared, that's all. Because my grandmother might not be—here."

"She might be dead, in there," Greg said. "Or sick. So we ought to see if anything's wrong with her. She hasn't actually moved away yet. There are curtains and rocking chairs and all."

Evie took the key from her pocketbook and put it in the keyhole. "It fits, all right."

She turned it, and the door swung open.

The hall was big, and the staircase did have stained glass in the window on the landing. But the carpet looked very ragged in spots, and when Evie hurried to the living room to look at the mirrored mantel, they saw that everything there also looked worn and shabby.

"It's the right mantel!" Evie said. "It looks like the one Mother was standing by in the picture!"

"Somehow," Greg said, frowning, "it doesn't seem like your grandma can be so very rich, Evie."

"You're right, Greg," Evie said slowly. "It sure doesn't. But—that's great! Really great! Don't you see? She's better than rich—she needs us! Mother can go back to her—we all can—if she's all alone and needs help. If she were still awfully rich, Mother would—if she gets well—still be too proud to come back like—

like the prodigal son, begging to be taken in again. But if her mother needs her, that's different. Maybe my grandmother really needs us! Oh, I hope she does!"

Ronny said, "Your hand—it's bleeding. Evie, don't hold that broken piece of stained glass so tight. It's cutting you."

"Let's see if it fits any place on the landing window." She wiped the blood on her shorts.

The boys let Evie go first, even though it was hard to stay behind a girl on a crutch. Ronny glanced up through the stained glass, and saw that beyond it the sky was indeed green and the tree leaves were red and blue. Just the way Christina had told Evie. And for a moment he could almost glimpse a little girl who looked something like Evie, only younger, playing with a doll and some doll furniture on the landing. But he knew she was just a ghost that wasn't really there.

Evie said slowly, "There's a broken place in one pane."

She reached toward it with the piece of stained glass in her hand, to try it in the place. Just as she said, in an awed voice, confirming what they all knew, "It fits —it's the right gingerbread house, all right—" they heard the front door open below them.

# Inside
# the Gingerbread House

They whirled around as a stern voice said, "What are you children doing in my house?"

Ronny thought, Let Evie tell her. His throat seemed paralyzed, and Greg was just standing, frozen.

But Evie moved. She moved back down the stairs with her crutch, her eyes on the lady who stood accusingly below them. The boys followed, hesitantly.

When Evie got to the next-to-last step, her eyes were on a level with the lady's face. It was a face, Ronny saw, marked with lines that looked like she'd done a lot of worrying. Her eyes were a little like Evie's— brown and troubled looking and yet wanting to hope. He wondered if when she cried her tears looked like

Evie's—if Evie had inherited those big, round, glassie tears. Family tears, like the family name.

She still hadn't answered the question. Now the lady repeated it. "What are you doing in my house?"

Evie straightened her shoulders, and Ronny wondered how she would find the right words. He hoped the lady wouldn't have a heart attack. After all, she didn't even know she had a granddaughter. But she didn't look so very old. She had gray hair, but she wasn't all bent over or anything. He calculated swiftly —she had to be at least sixty-five because of Uncle Sandy being older than Christina, but she could be any age after that. He guessed about sixty-five. Maybe she could stand the shock.

"What are you doing here? Answer me!"

Evie swallowed hard and said simply, "Grandmother, I've come home." She held out the piece of stained glass that fit the broken pane.

Mrs. Evelyn looked up at the window on the landing, and Ronny knew she saw the ghost child too. "Christina—" she whispered unbelievingly. "Oh, my child, my child—"

"Not Christina," Evie said. "I'm Evie. Evelyn. Her child. Your granddaughter."

Mrs. Evelyn didn't have a heart attack, but she did

grasp the newel post for something to hold onto. Evie stood waiting, her lips quivering.

Then her grandmother held out her arms and Evie tumbled into them, from the step, and Ronny knew everything was going to be all right.

It was, too. They sat down in the shabby living room and explained everything, Ronny doing most of the talking, Evie content just to sit nestled beside her grandmother on the sofa, with her grandmother's arm warm and loving around her, holding her close.

"So you come home with us, Mrs. Evelyn," Ronny said, "and see Joy, and Mama will take you to the hospital and maybe when Evie's mother sees you she'll get all right. She wanted to see you, so bad."

"She wanted to come home," Evie whispered. "All that time, she was wanting to come back."

"False pride," her grandmother said. "She should've known I'd want her home, no matter what happened."

"I guess that's what home means." Ronny thought it out. "A place where they want you no matter what you've done or what has happened to you. And you ought not ever be afraid to come back and admit you were wrong. Because it wouldn't make any difference."

"Not to a mother," Mrs. Evelyn said. "False pride hurts everybody—not only the one who's too proud. It hurts the people who love you, too. Especially a mother! Oh, Evie, Evie, I'm so glad you came home. I'm so glad you found me, before they tore down your mother's home."

She looked wonderingly at the little piece of broken stained glass. "And to think she kept that, all these years."

"She kept the jewelry, too," Evie reminded her. "And Mittens's tombstone and all."

At that, tears did roll down Mrs. Evelyn's face, and they were just like Evie's tears. I knew it, Ronny thought; she inherited them. I bet Christina cries like that too.

"Don't cry," he said. "You can buy another gingerbread house. If—if you have the money."

"They paid me for this place," Mrs. Evelyn said sadly. "I've probably got enough money. But I don't want another house. I want this one. I wanted to live in it till I died. This is home. My father's house he built for his bride. This is where Sandy and Christina grew up. Sandy used to ride on that banister out there on the porch when he was six—he called it his white horse. He named it Albino. Christina painted a picture of 'my house' when she was about six or seven. She used to call it hers and say she was going to live here all her life."

"We saved the picture," Greg told her. He patted her hand shyly.

Ronny felt like crying himself. It was so sad that she had to lose her home, where all her memories were.

But after all, now she had Christina back, and Evie and Joy. They could start some new memories for her.

Then he had his brilliant idea. "Hey!" he almost shouted. "I know what! You can take that money they paid you, and move your house! We saw one on the highway being moved somewhere else—whole. Why, yes'm, I bet you won't even have to take the furniture out. It was on wheels and a platform, the whole thing. Like on a great big trailer truck. See, Mrs. Evelyn, you don't have to lose the gingerbread house at all. And Christina can come home!"

Mrs. Evelyn looked stunned. Then she looked hopeful. Then she jumped up, almost dumping Evie off the sofa. "You may be right!" she said briskly. "What a clever idea, Ronny. It might really be possible! I wonder why I didn't think of that. But I've got to work fast. They're going to start tearing down this block next week. I'll call that real estate man who was trying to sell me a new house, and see if he has a lot to sell instead, and if he knows who can move a house. Oh, I wish I hadn't had the phone disconnected! But

I thought I had to move, this week. I came back today to start packing. Now—maybe I won't have to."

"You can use our phone," Ronny said. "Come on— it's nearly suppertime. And it's a long ride on the bus, and we have to transfer."

"I think I have enough money for a taxi," Mrs. Evelyn said. "When you're in a hurry to see your long-lost daughter and new grandbaby, I believe a taxi isn't extravagant."

Mama met them at the door with good news. "Your mother is conscious!" she called out to Evie, before she saw Mrs. Evelyn. "The hospital called. She wants to see you and Joy." Then she saw who was with them. "You found her! Oh, Evie, I'm so glad!"

"This is my friend, Mrs. Jameson," Evie introduced them, proudly. "This is my grandmother, Mrs. Evelyn." The way she said the name, Mrs. Evelyn, Ronny thought, made all their hard work worth while.

Mama actually put her arms around Mrs. Evelyn and hugged her. Ladies did seem to go in for a lot of that kind of stuff. It just meant they were glad, he supposed.

While Evie brought Joy for her grandmother to hold —there'd be some more hugging, that was sure— Ronny picked up the afternoon paper. There on the front page was a piece about the stolen-car ring. It said the police were about to close in on the two leaders, who were known to have come from California, and there were pictures of Finch and Crane Lewis and *WANTED* in big letters over the pictures.

Ronny smuggled the paper into his and Greg's room. He called Greg in and showed it to him, and Froman came too.

"We'd better hide it," Greg said, "so Evie won't have to worry about it while she's so glad about her grandma and her mother getting better and all. You know she said she sorta hoped he'd get away. So Joy's father wouldn't be in prison."

"Well, if we can keep her from reading the paper much, maybe she can think he did get away," Ronny said.

"Yeah. She won't be thinking about reading for a while, I guess. And Finch and Crane won't bother her mother much—this piece says they'll get about twenty years."

"Elementary, my dear Watson." He wadded the front page up into a ball and threw it to Froman, who cheerfully helped him tear it into little bits. Then he picked up the bits and went and flushed Finch and Crane Lewis down the toilet.

"You'll have to explain to Dad what happened to the front page," Greg predicted.

"Dad will understand," Ronny said. "And I bet he'll help Mrs. Evelyn get the gingerbread house moved, too."

When they went back into the living room, Evie was explaining to her grandmother about the mojo and why they would have to go and let her meet Aunt Riah, and tell Aunt Riah that Evie did have good luck. "I did—I found you!"

"That's my good luck," her grandmother said.

Evie said, "You need us." Her eyes were shining now, and not with tears.

"I certainly do."

Evie laughed, from pure happiness. "Mr. Holmes," she said to Ronny, "you and Dr. Watson sure solved The Case of the Missing Grandmother, all right. Thanks—Ron and Greg."

Ronny smiled at her, feeling suddenly shy, because old Evie was so grateful.

But Greg said solemnly, "Well, this whole thing has sure taught me a lesson. I'm not ever going to run away from home and get married."

**A suspenseful mystery with a surprise ending!**

## THE CHRISTMAS TREE MYSTERY

### by Wylly Folk St. John

Beth Carlton was in trouble. She accused Pete Abel of stealing the Christmas ornaments from her family tree, something
she knew he hadn't done. And what was worse—the police
believed her! Beth had two days to prove to the police that
Pete wasn't a thief, and all she had to go on was her step-
brother's word that Pete was innocent.

**An Avon Camelot Book**
**46300     $1.50**

# THE MIDNIGHT FOX

## by Betsy Byars

### illustrated by Ann Grifalconi

Tom didn't want to spend the summer on his Uncle's farm. But his parents were going to Europe and he had no choice.

One day, Tom saw the wild black fox and it was the most awesome sight he'd ever seen. He knew that his whole life, his whole world, would be changed. Then, during the most terrible night of his life, Tom had to find a way to save the wonderful black fox and her baby.

**An Avon Camelot Book**
**46987   $1.50**

*Also by Betsy Byars*
AFTER THE GOAT MAN   41590   $1.25
THE 18th EMERGENCY   46979   $1.50
RAMA THE GYPSY CAT   41608   $1.25
THE SUMMER OF THE SWANS   50526   $1.75
TROUBLE RIVER   47001   $1.50
THE WINGED COLT OF CASA MIA   46995   $1.50

Avon Camelot Books are available at your bookstore. Or, you may use Avon's special mail order service. Please state the title and code number and send with your check or money order for the full price, plus 50¢ per copy to cover postage and handling, to: AVON BOOKS, Mail Order Department, 224 West 57th Street, New York, New York 10019. Please allow 4-6 weeks for delivery.

# THE REAL ME
## by Betty Miles

"My book is not the kind that tells 'How Tomboy Mindy discovered that growing up gracefully can be as fun as playing baseball.'

"I have often thought how relaxing it would be to be invisible. But when I took over Richard's paper route they said 'girls can't deliver papers.' And when I wanted to take tennis instead of slimnastics, they said 'girls like to do graceful feminine things.' So I had to speak out. I only wanted things to be fair.

"My book is for anyone who might want to read about the life and thoughts of a person like me. If some boy wants to read this, go ahead. Maybe you will learn something."

**An Avon Camelot Book**
**48199    $1.50**

"Harold waited to see if he could catch sight of that glint of steel he was always hearing about. The gun barrel. He thought of how he must look standing there, fat and pale and scared. The perfect target . . ."

## AFTER THE GOAT MAN

### by Betsy Byars

### illustrated by Ronald Himler

When Harold played Monopoly with Ada and Figgy, he always won. He could make his voice sound deep and important on the phone. And he had a WCLG Golden Oldie T-shirt. But nothing could make up for the fact that he was fat. Harold thought he was the most miserable person in the world, until the night that Figgy's eccentric grandfather picked up a shotgun and disappeared.

Then, when Figgy was badly injured in an accident, it was suddenly up to Harold to find the Goat Man. And on the way, he discovered that his problems were very small compared with the problems of other people.

**An Avon Camelot Book**
**41590   $1.25**

**An old mansion, a graveyard, and a mysterious skull!**

# UNCLE ROBERT'S SECRET

## by Wylly Folk St. John

"You don't know what scared is till you've fallen out of a tree late at night into a bunch of broken-down gravestones, practically on top of somebody you think might be a mean guy . . . and there's an awful scream still ringing in your ears."

Bob should have known how hard it would be to keep a secret, especially when that secret happened to be a bedraggled little boy named Tim. And when Bob finally shared it with his brother and sister, they suddenly found themselves involved in a very spooky mystery.

**An Avon Camelot Book**
**46326    $1.50**

---

Dewey saw the Indian at the cabin door, hatchet in hand. A fear clutched him so great that he felt as if he were spinning around and falling ...

# TROUBLE RIVER

## by Betsy Byars

## illustrated by Rocco Negri

Twelve-year-old Dewey and his grandmother are all alone one night in their cabin when raiding Indians attack. They escape to the banks of Trouble River and cast off in Dewey's home-made raft.

So begins a dangerous journey—watching for Indians, finding the burned-out homesteads of their neighbors, and running over violent rapids—a breathtaking journey through fear.

**An Avon Camelot Book**
**47001   $1.50**

*Also by Betsy Byars*
THE SUMMER OF THE SWANS   50526   $1.75
AFTER THE GOAT MAN   41590   $1.25
THE MIDNIGHT FOX   46987   $1.50
RAMA THE GYPSY CAT   41608   $1.25
THE WINGED COLT OF CASA MIA   46995   $1.50

Avon Camelot Books are available at your bookstore. Or, you may use Avon's special mail order service. Please state the title and code number and send with your check or money order for the full price, plus 50¢ per copy to cover postage and handling, to: AVON BOOKS, Mail Order Department, 224 West 57th Street, New York, New York 10019. Please allow 4-6 weeks for delivery.

Gilly Ground was an orphan and all he wanted was a little peace and quiet . . .

## DORP DEAD

### by Julia Cunningham

### illustrated by James Spanfeller

Life in the orphanage was difficult in many ways. Gilly spent as much time as he could in the abandoned tower in the woods. It was peaceful there—and it was there that Gilly met the Hunter. Then, one day, he was placed in a foster home. And Gilly felt as though he were trapped in a nightmare come true.

**An Avon Camelot Book**
**51458   $1.95**

*Also by Julia Cunningham*
DEAR RAT   46615   $1.50

**Shipwrecked!**

# THE CAY

## by Theodore Taylor

All his life Philip had looked down upon black-skinned people. Now, suddenly, he was a refugee from a disastrous shipwreck and had to depend on an extraordinary black man named Timothy. There were just the two of them on the barren little Caribbean island . . . and a crack on the head had left Philip blind.

An exciting, moving adventure story, THE CAY tells of their struggle for survival . . . and of Philip's efforts to adjust to his blindness and to understand the dignified, wise, and loving man who was his companion.

**An Avon Camelot Book**
**31781   $1.50**